Secrets of Walnut Hill

RUTH FLANAGAN

ISBN 979-8-88540-586-7 (paperback)
ISBN 979-8-88540-587-4 (digital)

Copyright © 2022 by Ruth Flanagan

All rights reserved. No part of this publication may be reproduced, distributed, or transmitted in any form or by any means, including photocopying, recording, or other electronic or mechanical methods without the prior written permission of the publisher. For permission requests, solicit the publisher via the address below.

Christian Faith Publishing
832 Park Avenue
Meadville, PA 16335
www.christianfaithpublishing.com

Printed in the United States of America

Chapter 1

THE WARM BALMY AIR filled momentarily with smoke and dust as the train heaved and choked into action for the continued journey south. Laura found it necessary to turn her head and hold on to her small brimless toque to avoid the swirl of dust that kicked up around her. It seemed that everything and everyone in this part of the country was covered with a layer of endless dust.

When the dust settled, Laura turned toward the station, only to discover she was totally alone on the platform. Panic began to well up within her. Someone should have been waiting to meet her and take her the rest of the way to Walnut Hill. Had she been confused about the correct day? Could something have gone wrong?

Weary from her already arduous trip from Boston to Los Angeles, Laura sat on a nearby bench and carefully smoothed the skirt of her heliotrope taffeta dress, which was sadly showing the evidence of her journey. It had been a farewell gift from the family she worked for in Boston and was much fancier than she could ever afford. She hoped her beautiful outfit had not been ruined.

She reached into her handbag and retrieved Ian Castle's letter. Clearly, the letter stated her acceptance for the position of tutor for the three Castle children and instructed her to travel by train from Los Angeles to San Juan Capistrano, where she would be met and transported to his home on Friday, August 9, 1895. She folded the letter and returned it to her handbag.

Despite her weariness, the slight breeze from the sea was invigorating. Laura stood up and began to pace along the promenade so gracefully lined with archways common to the Spanish-influence architecture of the area. How strange and different this part of the country was from her home back in Boston. It was difficult to imagine that she was still in the same country. The rolling hillsides in the distance appeared devoid of any natural vegetation, yet they exuded a certain wildness, indicating they could withstand the buffeting winds which often came at them from the ocean.

Laura's parents had been killed during a severe storm at sea when she was only sixteen. She had then moved in with her Aunt Celia. Soon, it became apparent that she would have to seek employment in order to survive. Aunt Celia had not been a wealthy woman, and the burden of another body to feed and clothe was too great for her to handle.

Laura found a suitable position, teaching the young children of a prominent Boston family, and soon gained a reputation for her skills, particularly with children considered spoiled and difficult. However, the severe eastern winters began to take their toll on Laura. She was chronically ill, which threatened to affect her work with children.

Her doctor spoke many times of mineral springs in the west which were purported to "cure all one's ails," and it was this suggestion that prompted Laura to seek a job where she could take advantage of a warmer climate and explore the possible health benefits of a mineral springs spa. So when an ad appeared in a Boston newspaper offering a tutor's position for a family in San Juan Capistrano, California, Laura mailed an application. Much to her surprise, she was accepted based solely on exchanges of correspondence with Mr. and Mrs. Castle.

Light was fading as dusk settled over the small western town. A deep sense of desperation and loneliness swept over Laura. She was alone in a strange place with no idea how to contact her new employer. Unwelcome tears filled her eyes. Just then, she spotted a small horse-drawn wagon coming toward the train station platform.

An elderly bent man wearing a sombrero climbed down and walked toward her.

"Senorita Palmer?" he asked. "I am Manuel. I work for Mr. Castle, and he sent me to pick you up. I apologize for my tardiness. Let me help you with your bags."

The old man struggled with Laura's trunks, then helped her up into the wagon. With a gentle slap of the reins, the horse slowly plodded away from the station. It was nearly dark, making it difficult for Laura to distinguish the buildings or what direction they were traveling. A building near the station had a sign indicating it to be a cannery.

The giant shadow of the mission loomed behind them as they turned to head out of town. Laura had heard about the mission and hoped to visit the ruins when she could. Much of the mission had been destroyed years before by an earthquake, but the ruins still held a fascination for visitors interested in the history of its foundation.

"Is it far to where the Castles live?" Laura asked.

"Not far. We should be there soon."

"Are Mr. and Mrs. Castle good people to work for?"

"Si. Senor Ian is a good boss. His mother, Mrs. Castle, is a fine lady. But I do not work for her."

"Oh, so Mrs. Castle is Ian's mother?"

"Si."

"What is it you do for Mr. Castle?"

"I help with the walnuts and do small jobs around the place." With that, Manuel appeared to have nothing more to say.

After a few more unsuccessful attempts at conversation, Laura decided her questions would have to wait. Manuel did not appear to be predisposed to long bouts of talking. Laura instead turned her thoughts to what her new home would be like. She had read that the walnut industry had originated in this valley in 1870 and continued to be a primary crop ever since. Walnut Hill was considered to be one of the biggest orchards in Capistrano, and Ian Castle was considered a very influential man.

After what seemed an eternity to Laura's aching bones, Manuel turned the wagon off the main road and proceeded up a hill toward an imposing, pompous Victorian structure which was in obvious contrast to the low adobe buildings of the town. In the late twilight, Walnut Hill appeared like a giant yellow cat grinning down on the surrounding valley.

As the wagon drew up in front of the double-wide front steps, the grin, caused by light shining through the white spindle supports of the verandah, took on the appearance of an austere smirk. At the corner of the house, a square tower reached above the roof in a pointed spire. Except for the light that came from the front entrance, the house was dark and seemingly uninhabited.

A plump woman wearing a colorful tiered skirt came out onto the verandah to meet them. Manuel helped Laura down from the wagon seat and introduced her to his wife Consuela, the housekeeper at Walnut Hill.

"The senorita must be very tired from such a long journey," Consuela said. "Come, I have prepared some food for you."

It was true. Laura was beginning to feel the strain of her trip, but as Manuel and Consuela exchanged a few brief comments in Spanish, she had a deeper sense that something was wrong and she could contain her curiosity no longer.

"Consuela, where is Mr. Castle and where are the children?"

"So many questions on an empty stomach. First, you will eat, then there will be time for talking."

Consuela led the way into the front entry hall. An elegant leaded cathedral glass lantern hung overhead. Little stars cut into the ruby glass twinkled their reflection onto the gleaming polished wood floor. A low bench sat stiff-backed against the right wall, and a stairway curved gently to the left. Aside from that, the entry was completely devoid of ornamentation.

Manuel disappeared up the stairs with Laura's trunks. Consuela indicated that Laura should follow her down the hall toward the back of the house. Laura noticed several closed doors along the hallway and wondered what lay behind each one. A strange foreboding overcame her. Walnut Hill seemed to hold some sort of strange secret which hung over the entire household like a blanket. For the first time since she left Boston, Laura wondered if she had made a big mistake in accepting this position.

After enjoying a tasty bowl of soup that contained meatballs, Laura was shown to her room. She undressed quickly and allowed her weary body to sink into the soft comfort of the bed. Almost immediately, she fell asleep. Her questions would have to wait.

Chapter 2

SUNLIGHT EXTENDED WELL INTO the room when Laura finally awoke the next morning. Unwilling to subject her stiff, aching body to any undue movement, she nestled against the warmth of the bed. From this vantage point, she surveyed the room which she had been too weary to notice the night before. The position of the sun streaming through the windows told her she was in the tower at the southwest corner of the house.

Across the room from the bed were two long narrow windows topped with decorative leaded glass in patterns of pale blue. Heavy dark-blue drapes were pulled back over sheer white ninon curtains. Blue cornflowers against a field of white covered the walls, and the dark blue of the drapes was repeated in the bed coverlet. The varying shades of blue gave a cooling effect to the room, which obviously caught much of the morning and afternoon sunlight.

Directly in front of the two long windows, matching side chairs with light-blue velvet seats sat on either side of a round tea table. A small chiffonier stood along the wall next to the door. The only other furniture was a large wardrobe cupboard where Consuela had hung her clothes and the massive ornately carved bed where Laura now languished.

A pitcher and basin had been placed on the chiffonier. Slowly, Laura eased herself out of bed, poured some water into the basin, and began washing off the dust from her long trip. Her long auburn hair was a disheveled mess from sleeping. She brushed it vigorously to unsnarl it, then fastened it loosely at the nape of her neck with two tortoiseshell combs.

From the wardrobe cupboard, she chose a plain brown skirt and an unbleached muslin blouse with puffed sleeves and high collarless neckline. Laura considered herself rather plain looking with a too prominent nose, but her striking auburn hair combined with a sprinkling of freckles across her nose and cheeks gave her appearance a friendliness which most people warmed to immediately.

Refreshed and ready to explore her new surroundings, Laura left her room and walked down the sweeping staircase. At the landing on the second floor, she noticed a door on the right and wondered what was beyond it since the family's quarters appeared to be to her left. In the daylight, the inside of the house, which had seemed so austere from the outside, now seemed to evoke a certain elegance of design.

Across the hall from the stairway, double doors were closed on what Laura imagined was the parlor. She pictured a regal setting of dark woods and rich red velvets. Out of curiosity, she opened the doors to have a look. Instead of grand and graceful furnishings, the room was practically devoid of any furniture at all.

A couple of dusty leather chairs stood by the fireplace, and a writing desk had been placed in the corner by a window. At the other end of the long room stood a trestle dining table with six matching chairs set on a faded Oriental rug. The rest of the room was cluttered with children's games, papers, and toys. Quickly, she closed the doors and proceeded down the hall toward the kitchen.

Consuela greeted Laura with a plate of scrambled eggs and small sausages. Steam rose from a platter of warmed tortillas that had been buttered and rolled into long finger shapes. Laura realized she was really quite hungry and ate voraciously. She couldn't help noticing, however, that Consuela was unusually silent and seemed preoccupied. She kept glancing out the kitchen window as though she was expecting something to happen or someone to appear.

"Consuela."

The Mexican woman was startled by the sound of another's voice.

"I'm sorry. I didn't mean to startle you," Laura said.

"It is nothing," Consuela replied. "My mind is miles away today. Did you have a question?"

I have a hundred questions, Laura thought. But she said, "I was just wondering what kind of soup that was last night. It was quite delicious."

"That is called *albondigas,* a Mexican meatball soup."

"I noticed some disarray in the parlor. It is in such contrast to the lovely room where I am staying. Why is my room so beautifully decorated, but the parlor seems to have been totally neglected? Did something happen in there?"

"The room where you are staying used to be the master bedroom and was decorated by Senora Maria," Consuela began. "Since her death, Senor Ian does not seem to care as much for fancy things."

"But surely...," Laura began.

Consuela definitely was uncomfortable with the questioning and reluctant to engage in any further conversation. She collected Laura's empty plate and continued washing dishes. Laura decided she better drop the subject for the time being and said, "Since the children are not here and I cannot begin their lessons, could I have a look around and get familiar with my new home?"

"What do you mean by 'look around'?"

"I have nothing sinister in mind, I assure you. I just meant that I would like to see the room I shall be using to teach the children, maybe set up a few things I brought with me. And if permitted, I should like to look around outside. This part of the country is all so new to me."

Consuela seemed to relax and warmed toward Laura. "You must excuse me, senorita. I am not always so distraught. The last couple of days have been very trying, and I am very tired."

"Just what has been happening the past couple of days?" Once again, Consuela stiffened and fell silent. Obviously, the woman was not going to share any family secrets with a stranger from back east. Laura would just have to wait to get the answers to all her questions.

"I think I'll just go for a walk to get acquainted with my new home."

"That is a good idea," Consuela replied, not trying to hide her relief to be rid of Laura's questioning. "Take this old straw hat for protection. The sun is very hot, and your skin is so fair."

Laura took the hat and walked out onto the back veranda. It was only midmorning, yet she could already feel the heat penetrate her clothing. While she tried to decide which direction to choose for her walk, she became aware that the same lack of caring was evident outside as well.

She made a mental note to ask Mr. Castle if she might plant some flower beds around the house. There appeared to be little or no natural vegetation in this barren countryside. She knew that even the large eucalyptus trees had been brought from Australia and planted there, apparently as a windbreak for the less sturdy walnut trees.

Laura's gaze went out beyond the few small adobe outbuildings to the hillsides beyond. Though graceful and rolling in appearance, they were denuded by nature. No stately trees dotted the horizon, only the endless sweep of the hillside.

The walnut industry that had begun in the Capistrano Valley produced walnuts that were being compared to those of the Riviera and Malaga in the south of France. Laura decided to investigate the walnut grove. Passing by a shed which wasn't really a shed but merely a roof supported by heavy posts, she noticed Manuel and a couple of the Mexican workers spreading walnuts in a single layer to dry. She waved to Manuel and continued toward the grove.

It was cooler in the shade of the walnut trees, some of which appeared to be forty or fifty feet high and just about as wide. Laura ran her hand along the smooth gray bark of one of the trees and thought how different it was from the shaggy loose bark of the eucalyptus tree. Because it was nearly fall, the husks were beginning to open, and nuts were dropping to the ground. Stooping to pick up a walnut, Laura removed a piece of remaining husk and tried to crack open the thin shell. Since it had not yet been dried, it was not brittle enough to crack easily. She slipped it into her pocket to be dealt with later.

As Laura neared the other side of the grove, she caught a glimpse of a small adobe cottage that lay beyond the trees. Suddenly, she heard voices coming from the cottage. She was not close enough to hear the words being spoken, but it was apparent someone was having a heated argument. Just as she was about to knock on the door to the cottage, it opened, and a dark-haired boy of about fifteen ran past her, causing her to jump out of his way.

A matronly woman wearing an apron over a lovely brown-and-white-striped muslin dress with mutton leg sleeves appeared in the doorway and, looking at Laura, said, "I must apologize for my grandson. He has quite a temper at times. Won't you come in for a few minutes and meet the girls? They spent the night with me while everyone was out looking for the boy."

"Thank you so much. I've been wondering where the children were, but the lovely Mexican couple seemed reluctant to tell me anything."

"Yes, well…I'm Fiona Castle, and I'm the one who convinced my son to hire you. I can see already my judgment was spot on. Come have some tea and meet Bridget and Cassie. You'll have to wait a bit, I'm afraid, to formally meet Reuben."

Two polite girls dressed in matching dresses topped with white pinafores curtsied to her. "Hello, Miss Palmer," they said in unison.

"Please call me Laura."

"Papa would never let us do that," said the younger of the two, twirling her finger around her strawberry-blond ringlets. "It would not be polite. My name is Bridget, and I'm six."

"Well, Bridget, do you think he would approve of your calling me Miss Laura?"

"Yes, I think he might allow that," said the serious older one, nodding her blond braids. "I'm Cassie."

"How old are you, Cassie?"

"I'll be twelve in May."

"I'm pleased to meet you both. I look forward to our spending time together and getting to know one another better." It was clear to Laura that Cassie was very protective of Bridget and watched over her in a motherly fashion.

Chapter 3

LAURA RETURNED TO THE house with Bridget and Cassie, and while they went to put away their things in their room, she headed to the parlor. Just as she was about to turn the knob to enter the disheveled room, the door suddenly was yanked open and she stumbled into the arms of her new employer.

"Miss Palmer, I presume." Ian Castle helped her right herself and held her at arm's length. His eyes filled with an apparent rage at odds with his well-dressed demeanor.

"I'm so sorry," Laura stammered. "I didn't—"

"That's quite all right," he said, his soft voice not at all matching the fury she had just witnessed in his eyes. "I'm afraid I was in a bit of a hurry when I opened the door."

Gathering her composure, Laura faced the man whose eyes now sparkled with a bit of humor. "I was hoping to run into you, sir. Well, so to speak, that is. Could we sit down and discuss my employment and what my duties are to be?"

"Naturally, we will need to do that, but I'm afraid that I have a matter of some urgency to attend to at the moment."

"Sir, if I may be blunt, I have a lot of questions, and well, Manuel and Consuela have been very vague."

"I apologize for this rather unorthodox beginning to your stay, but I will be able to answer any questions you may have when I return. For now, why don't you visit with my daughters until I return?"

Just then, the girls came downstairs and were standing in the hallway.

"Here they are now. Let me introduce you."

"We already met Miss Laura over at Grannie's," Bridget said.

"Well, I'll leave you to get better acquainted," Ian said, and doffing his bowler hat, he quickly left by the back door.

Both girls looked to Laura to see what they should do next. Laura cautiously opened the door to the parlor and motioned them inside. She located a child-sized chair that was overturned and took it to a small table so that she could sit with the girls.

"So why don't you tell me a little bit about yourselves? Let's start with what you do for fun or what is your favorite subject to study."

"I like to color," Bridget volunteered. "But I can't always stay in the lines."

"Ah, a budding artist, eh? What about you, Cassie? What do you like to do?"

"I don't do anything much, I guess, Miss Palmer," Cassie said, ignoring the plan to refer to her as Miss Laura.

"She likes to draw, and Mama taught her how to embroider before she went to be with God," Bridget explained.

Cassie scowled at her younger sister as though she had just aired the family's dirty laundry to a complete stranger.

"Do you have a piece you could show me?" Laura was determined to break through the icy barrier Cassie seemed to have built around herself.

"I have some things in my room, but Papa said we should stay here until he comes back."

"Well, maybe you could show me some other time."

"Miss Laura, is it true you are going to make us study all day long and never let us have any fun?" Bridget asked.

Laura chuckled. "It's true I have been hired to be your teacher, but I wouldn't say we won't have some fun doing it. Don't you like schoolwork?"

"We haven't had much school teaching," Cassie said. "Mama did some while she was here, but since she died, Papa hasn't had much time to spend on teaching."

Laura wondered about public school, but before she could voice her question, her thoughts were interrupted by the sounds of loud shouting coming from outside the house.

"It's Reuben," squealed Bridget, jumping up from her chair and running to the corner window. Laura rose from her chair and followed Bridget to the window. In the yard, Ian Castle was vehemently scolding the boy she had seen running from the cottage near the walnut grove. Although she could not hear what was being said, it was apparent from his rigid stance and his attempts to interrupt that the boy was not the least bit repentant.

"Reuben's in trouble again," Bridget volunteered.

"What kind of trouble?" Laura asked.

"He ran away again last night."

That certainly explains why no one was on hand to meet my train, Laura thought, *and why everyone was acting so mysteriously.*

As Laura watched the scene between father and son unfold, she observed Fiona emerge from the trees and wrap her arms protectively around Reuben. She began to argue with Ian who threw up his arms in frustration and turned to stomp off to the drying sheds. The woman and boy walked slowly toward the house, seemingly deep in conversation.

Bridget suddenly ran from the room, followed closely by Cassie. Laura followed them in the hope of finding out what was going on.

"This must be Reuben," Laura said as they entered the kitchen. "I'm pleased to meet you."

Reuben bowed his head as he nodded slowly. He appeared quite uncomfortable in the presence of his tutor. His grandmother gave him a quick slap on the backside and sent him upstairs to his room. "I'll be up in a moment, and we will talk," she explained.

"I was hoping to spend some time with all three children today to see where we need to start with their lessons." Laura was disappointed that Reuben had been dismissed so quickly.

"I'm afraid Reuben has been disobedient and will have to suffer his punishment today. You may work with the girls, if you like." With that, the woman followed in the direction Reuben had gone. Laura looked at Bridget and Cassie. "Why don't we take a walk?"

Bridget was visibly excited, while Cassie seemed to acquiesce for lack of anything better. Consuela appeared just then and explained that lunch would be waiting for them when they returned from their walk. The girls grabbed their sunbonnets and raced out the door, eager to be out of the house. Laura donned the hat she had worn earlier and joined the girls outside.

"Where shall we go?" Laura asked.

"Let's go up that hill over there," Bridget pointed. "You can see the ocean from up there."

"What a splendid idea," Laura said. "But that looks like quite a long walk."

"Afraid you can't go that far?" Cassie asked.

"I was just concerned whether we would be back in time for lunch."

"We can make it if you can." Cassie began running.

"I'll stay and walk with you if you like." Bridget reached up and put her hand in Laura's.

"Thank you, Bridget. That's very kind of you. But if you would like to run like Cassie, it's all right with me."

"Really?" Bridget's eyes widened. "You wouldn't mind?"

"Of course not. Go ahead."

Bridget's ringlets flew behind her as she attempted to catch up with her sister. Laura continued along the path the girls had taken. She wondered what it must be like for these children growing up in a place where they could just take off across the fields without a care in the world. Her own childhood had been so structured and restricted in the city that she couldn't help being just a little envious of the freedom the Castle children enjoyed.

She labored up the last few feet to the top of the hillside where the girls stood looking off into the distance. Laura could not believe her eyes as she stared at the panorama in front of her. For as far as she could see in any direction, the brown hills rippled and tumbled in their haste to meet the sea. Although they were still probably five miles or so from the point where land actually touched the water, it was as though Laura could feel being at one with the ocean. As she stood looking out at the horizon, she suddenly became aware, for the first time, that the earth really was round. She pointed out the curved arc of the horizon to the girls and explained how many centuries before, people had believed the world was flat.

"Everybody knows that Christopher Columbus proved they were wrong," Cassie interjected.

"Actually it was the ancient Greeks who first discovered the earth was round," instructed Laura, not wanting to miss a chance to educate the girls. "The myth that Columbus proved the earth was not flat was invented in 1828 when Washington Irving wrote a story about *The Life and Voyages of Christopher Columbus.* He made up the part about Columbus setting out to prove the earth was round."

Cassie nodded.

"Why? Have you never noticed the curved horizon before now?" she asked.

"Living in the city as I have all my life, I never actually realized you could see how the earth curves."

"Did you like living in a city?" Bridget asked.

"Well, I did while I was there, but that is because I never knew that anything like this existed."

"I want to go to San Diego when I grow up," Cassie announced.

"Me too," Bridget said.

"Oh, you don't know anything about it," Cassie began to sulk again. "You only say 'me too' because I said it was what I wanted."

"And what do you know of this city?" Laura tried to pull Cassie back into the conversation. "Have you been there?"

"No. But mommy told me stories of when she lived there and of the grand balls and the fancy shops. I will live there someday."

"Then your mother was not from around here?"

"Mommie came from Mexico when she was a young girl. She lived in a beautiful house by the sea." Cassie held her head majestically. "Then, she met my father and moved here."

Laura could not overlook the gesture Cassie made as she then lowered her head when she spoke of her father, and it was not lost on her that the girl had called him father as opposed to the usual use of the form—papa.

"And your grandmother lives here too?"

"When Granddad Castle died, Mommie insisted she come to live with us. She did not want to be in the way in our house, so father built her the small adobe cottage on the other side of the orchard."

"That's where Reuben goes when he wants to get away from Papa."

"Bridget, be quiet."

The subject of Reuben seemed to be like an open wound, and Laura decided it was best not to pursue it any further with them. She did, however, plan to speak to Mr. Castle about the boy. Too many questions remained unanswered.

"It's time we head back to the house, girls. Consuela must have lunch ready by now."

The girls raced in the direction of the house, leaving Laura to make her way back alone. What a strange household she found herself in. There were so many unanswered questions, and even the children seemed to have secrets. She could not help but wonder what went on in this home and how on earth she was going to fit in.

Laura was deep in thought as she stopped to pick some wildflowers and did not, at first, hear the approaching horse. Just as she was about to step onto the path that led to the house, the horse and rider sped past her and turned toward the drying sheds.

"Of all the nerve!" Laura exclaimed to no one in particular. "That has to be the rudest person in the valley."

Laura continued on toward the house. Bridget and Cassie had already washed up and were seated at the table waiting for her. Quickly, she removed her hat and went to the sink to wash her hands.

"Did you see that rude rider? He nearly knocked me down."

"No, senorita, I did not see. I have been busy with the girls and with getting lunch on the table. Please sit down."

Consuela served individual salads made with a corn tortilla covered with refried beans and topped with lettuce and tomatoes, which she called a tostada. Laura was unaccustomed to the strange name and combination of food but found that it was not at all objectionable. Just as they were finishing their tostadas, they heard boots stomping up the back steps. A man's voice called out. "Hullo."

Consuela rose from the table and went to open the back door. "Ah, Senor Dylan, it is only you."

"Si, Consuela. I have come to take you away with me."

"Senor Dylan, you are a crazy one." Consuela swatted at him and laughed.

"Actually, I came to apologize to the lovely young lady I nearly ran over a while ago."

"Come on in. Senorita Laura Palmer," Consuela said as Laura rose, "this crazy gringo is Dylan Laughlin from the Valencia Rancho."

Chapter 4

A STRIKING SIX-FOOT MAN WEARING jeans and chaps, holding his hat in his hand, stepped forward to shake Laura's hand, which she extended reluctantly. Laura felt the warmth of blush on her face as she stared into the piercing blue eyes that peered at her from above a bushy mustache.

"I'm so sorry if I frightened you," Dylan said. "I was not looking where the horse was headed because my mind was on the message I needed to deliver to Ian."

"What message?" Consuela asked.

"Some thieves robbed the store in town, and I thought Ian might want to join the posse to go after them."

Laura could understand the urgency of his mission but still was not sure why it had been necessary to ride so close to where she was walking. She still thought him to be a very rude man. However, she decided it best to accept his apology rather than make a scene.

"I accept your apology, but you should be more careful where you are going. The next time, it could be one of these girls that you try to bowl over."

Dylan struggled to hide a brief smile. He admired her spunk and did not want to antagonize her any further by seeming to find her abruptness amusing. With a quick nod of his head, Dylan put his hat back on, turned, and began to leave.

"I need to get back out to see if Ian is saddled up and ready to go." And with that, he left.

"What do you think of our Mr. Dylan?" Consuela asked. "Is he not a very handsome man?"

"I suppose you could say he was handsome, and I am quite sure he maintains that opinion of himself. But he seems a bit rough around the edges if you ask me."

"Don't you like Dylan?" Bridget asked.

"I really don't know him well enough to form an opinion one way or the other, I guess. Why don't we talk about what we can do this afternoon? Maybe we could busy ourselves with setting the parlor in order so that we can study tomorrow."

"Daddy will want Reuben to clean the mess in the parlor. After all, he's the one who messed it up." Cassie frowned.

"Perhaps I should talk to your father and suggest we all pitch in so that we can use that room for your schoolwork."

With that, the conversation turned to talk of trivial things with Consuela offering an opinion now and then. Laura noticed the housekeeper seemed to be a bit reserved and would not look directly at Laura, simply focusing on the children instead.

When they had finished eating, Consuela announced it was time for the girls to lie down for a little siesta. Laura began to protest, but Consuela informed her it was customary for the girls to nap in the afternoon and that it might be a good idea if Laura would lie down to rest for a bit. Laura decided the housekeeper was right and a little nap might be refreshing. Perhaps when she woke, Mr. Castle would have returned and they could finally sit down and have a meaningful conversation, one that would provide some clue as to what was going on.

On the way to her room, Laura stopped to have a look into the room at the landing, but when she turned the doorknob, she discovered the door was locked. Continuing on to her room, Laura felt too restless to lie down, so she sat at the table near the window. She decided to work on creating some sort of lesson plan for the children that she could present to Mr. Castle to show him she was earnest in her endeavor to teach the children. Before she got very far in her planning, the afternoon sun shining through the window began to make her drowsy. Finally, she gave up lesson planning and lay on the bed coverlet and promptly fell asleep.

Laura had no idea how long she had been asleep, but the sun was fading as loud voices disturbed her. Obviously, Mr. Castle had returned and another row had erupted. Laura ran a brush through her hair, rearranged the combs holding it, and proceeded downstairs to see what the fuss was all about this time. As she neared the bottom of the stairs, she ran into Reuben who was storming up to his room after yet another admonishment.

"What on earth is going on?" Laura asked as she rounded the stairs where she found Ian Castle standing with both hands on his hips and looking quite dour.

"Ah, Miss Palmer. I guess I owe you some explanations. Please step into my study, won't you?"

Ian Castle indicated a door to his left; and Laura slowly stepped into an austere room, which held a large rolltop desk, a few bookcases, and a couple of side chairs but little else. Again, Laura was astounded at the lack of personal touches. After the beautiful furnishings in her room, the stark contrast to what she had seen of the rest of the house was puzzling to say the least.

"Please take a seat here," Ian motioned to one of the side chairs. "I will attempt to answer as many of your questions as I can."

"I'm not sure where to begin," Laura said. "There seems to be a problem between you and your son that is keeping this entire household on edge. I can't help but wonder what has happened between you."

"Without revealing any personal information regarding my family, let me just say that Reuben is a rebellious child and has caused me and his mother an enormous amount of grief."

"I thought your wife had passed away?"

"Yes, Maria died a couple of years ago. Since then, Reuben has become more and more belligerent and willful."

"Perhaps he misses his mother and is acting out as a means of coping with his grief. How did your wife die? What happened?"

For a moment, Laura thought Ian would not answer her question. He bowed his head and nearly laid it down on the desktop.

He slowly began to raise his head and looked to Laura as though he might start crying at any moment.

"I had gone to Santa Ana on business. The girls and Reuben were staying with their grandmother in the small cottage. My wife was alone in the house since Manuel and Consuela had gone to town to pick up supplies." He coughed into his hand as though to clear his throat. "When I returned, I found my wife lying on the verandah. She was not breathing, but I sent for the doctor anyway. There was nothing he could do. She was gone."

"And you have no idea what happened to her?"

"She had been shot, and there were signs of a struggle but no indication with whom she had struggled."

"Well, that could certainly explain why Reuben would be so upset. To have been so nearby and not be able to prevent what happened."

Ian stood and began trying to usher Laura out of the room. "I think that is enough explanations for now. You may go."

"But I wanted to talk to you about the lessons I have planned and ask you if we could straighten the parlor to make a kind of classroom for the children."

"Since tomorrow is Sunday and the family will be attending church, I have instructed Reuben to begin clearing the mess in the parlor on Monday. You are free to do as you will as far as the children's lessons are concerned. Just be aware that Reuben will do all he can to disrupt whatever you plan." With that, Ian closed the door to his office, leaving Laura standing in the hall with her mouth slightly open in protest.

It was impossible for Laura to decide whether she would ever get along with her new employer. One minute, he seemed totally charming, and the next, he was just short of being rude. Shaking her head in dismay, Laura headed into the kitchen where she found Manuel sitting at the table while Consuela busied herself with dinner preparations.

"Have the girls gotten up from their siesta yet?" Laura asked.

"Oh, si. They have gone to the cottage to spend some time with their abuela," Consuela answered. "They will be back in time for dinner."

"Abuela?" Laura looked puzzled.

"Their grandmother," said Consuela.

"I think I am going to turn out to be the student here, what with learning all the rules and customs and trying to understand the Spanish names for things."

"I'm sure you will catch on quickly," Consuela assured her. "Give yourself a few days to settle in, and it will all seem second nature soon."

Laura turned to Manuel and asked, "Did you find the men who robbed the store?"

"No, we lost their trail down near San Juan Point. Looks like they went into the ocean."

"Why would they go into the ocean?" Consuela asked.

"I don't think they did, but that is where their trail seemed to disappear."

"Does this sort of thing happen often?" Laura asked. "Do thieves come to this area often? Was it thieves that shot Mrs. Castle? Should we be concerned about thieves here?"

"No, senorita. These thieves do not seem to have a taste for walnuts. And I don't think whoever shot Senora Castle came back to rob a store."

About that time, a commotion could be heard on the back porch. The door to the kitchen opened, and Bridget came bounding through, followed closely by Cassie and Fiona.

"The girls have been telling me that you are going to be a stern teacher who won't let them have any fun."

"I'm afraid my sternness has been greatly exaggerated. I prefer to teach in a gentle manner."

"That is what your former employer indicated when I asked for references. I'm sure you will do an excellent job making young ladies out of these two. Reuben, on other hand, may require a heavier hand. His willfulness is getting a little out of control."

"Perhaps it was his mother's death that has him in turmoil."

"Yes, perhaps, but that occurred quite a while ago. He should be accepting the fact that she is gone."

Laura opened her mouth to say something but was interrupted as Reuben came bursting into the room, obviously abandoning his self-exile.

"I know she is gone. What I don't know is who is responsible for her death. And nobody seems to care enough to try and find out."

"Now, Reuben…" His grandmother reached to console him, but he pulled away from her.

"When's dinner, Consuela? I'm starved!" Reuben asked.

"If you go get washed up, we can get the table set and eat as soon as your father finishes in his office."

Consuela turned to Bridget and Cassie. "Why don't you two wash up, then come help me set the table?"

"That's my cue to head back to my cottage," Fiona said as she turned to leave.

"Don't you eat with the family?" Laura looked puzzled.

"Not unless there is a special occasion or a celebration. I like to keep my life as separate as I can so as to not interfere with theirs."

With that, she left while Laura couldn't help wondering just how much she didn't interfere.

Chapter 5

MONDAY MORNING, LAURA BEGAN working with Bridget and Cassie to clean up the parlor and to arrange a sort of classroom. She even managed to convince Reuben to lend a hand by telling him she needed his help. When she complained about the starkness of the room and wondered out loud how she was ever going to make a classroom out of what there was, Reuben said he might have an idea.

"I want to show you something," Reuben said, taking her hand and leading her into the hallway.

"What are you up to now?" asked Laura.

Reuben reached behind a cupboard door and produced a set of keys. He then asked Laura to follow him upstairs. At the landing, he put a key into the locked door that Laura had tried before, opening it onto an open-air porch. He then used another key to unlock the door into a room off the porch and stepped aside to allow Laura to enter.

Laura gasped as she found herself standing in a room filled with lush vegetation, bookshelves along one wall, and the nearly floor-to-ceiling windows she had spied from outside. There were several white wicker chairs and a settee covered in a pale blue-and-yellow floral print arranged for comfortable seating. A book lie open on a small table as though someone had just put it down and gone to fetch something.

"What is this room?"

"It was my mother's solarium. She used to bring us here to sit and read with her. I always loved being here with her."

Laura could definitely see a woman's touch that was so missing in the parlor. "So why is it locked up now? Shouldn't you still be enjoying this lovely space?"

"Papa closed it up and locked it when she died. Consuela is the only one allowed in here, but I found where she hides the keys. This is where I hide sometimes when they think I've run away."

Laura was moved by the boy's sadness yet proud of his ingenuity. "I am going to speak to your father about allowing us to use this as your classroom. It is perfect for that and should be used."

Suddenly, they were startled by a sound from the doorway. "What do you think you are doing in here!" bellowed Ian. "This room is off-limits. How did you even get in here?"

"I…I'm sorry, sir," Reuben stuttered. "It is my fault. I knew where the keys were and brought Miss Laura here."

Wondering why he had returned to the house unexpectedly, Laura explained, "I was looking for a more suitable place for a classroom, and Reuben was kind enough to risk punishment to show me this room. It would make a perfect classroom."

"This room was my wife's sanctuary, and everything is as she left it. No one is permitted in here with the exception of Consuela who comes in to dust and water the plants. I would appreciate your staying out of here. Now go! Reuben, I will deal with you later."

"Please do not punish Reuben, sir. I am the one who is responsible."

Ian stepped to one side and, with a sweeping gesture, indicated they should leave. Laura decided to take a stand despite Ian's obvious agitation. "Sir, I implore you to consider allowing me to use this space as a classroom for the children. Why the books alone in here could provide a wealth of information for them. It is such a bright, sunny place just meant to be used."

"Miss Palmer, I do not take kindly to being spoken to in that manner."

"No, sir, I'm sure you are not. But you hired me to give your children an education, and I believe the solarium provides an atmosphere much more conducive to learning than the stark bleakness of a corner of the parlor."

From the look on Ian's face, Laura was certain she was about to be fired, but at least she had said what she believed. Ian stood silently for a moment and then with a curt nod said, "Very well then. I can see you have made your point. You may use the solarium for your classes, but I will not tolerate any tomfoolery or destructive activity in here."

"Thank you very much, sir. The children will be so delighted."

With that, Ian turned and left Laura and Reuben sharing a smile. They in turn left, closed the door, and locked it behind them.

*****

Laura enjoyed working with the girls. Bridget was always so cheery and bouncy, while Cassie's sullenness began to wear off and Laura could see she was a very bright young girl. Reuben still felt it necessary to prove what a problem he could be, but Laura was determined to break through his rough, tough exterior. She could see there was a sad young boy inside who needed some special attention and guidance. Hopefully, she would be able to get close enough to him to find out what bothered him so much and why he and his father could not get along.

After a few days, Laura felt ready to begin some classes with the girls. She decided to concentrate on reading, mathematics, and art to begin with. Bridget struggled with reading but with practice could do fairly well for someone her age. She was not very adept with numbers, however, and would require a lot of work in that area. Cassie excelled at everything, including being an excellent artist.

On the day of art class, Reuben wandered into the solarium to see what the girls were doing. He laughed at Bridget's attempt to color and appeared slightly jealous of Cassie's pencil drawing.

"I could do better than that," Reuben announced, looking over Cassie's shoulder.

"Well, why don't you then?" Cassie countered.

"Ah, drawing is for girls. Men don't draw."

"Some of the most famous artists are men. In fact, most of them are men," Laura explained.

"Yeah, like who?"

"Have you ever heard of Leonardo da Vinci or Michelangelo? They are considered masters in the art world. Da Vinci was also an inventor."

"I could invent things."

"I bet you could. Why don't you invent something and bring it to me next week when we have art class?"

Reuben grumbled something about maybe he would just do that and slammed the door as he left the classroom. Laura smiled as she thought about what he might invent, for she was sure that next week, he would be in art class to show off his invention.

"Why don't we go outside for a nature walk? It's a beautiful day, and we shouldn't spend all of it indoors."

"What's a nature walk?" Bridget asked.

"Well, we can make it anything we want it to be. We could walk back up to the top of the hill and look at the ocean, or we could talk about what kind of flowers would look nice around the edge of the veranda or wander in the walnut grove and discuss walnuts or—"

"Sounds kind of dumb to me," said Cassie.

"You never want to do anything fun. You just want to read and draw," pouted Bridget.

"If you would like to take a book along to read while we sit on the hilltop, that's fine. Or bring your sketchbook so that you can draw a picture of what we see on our walk."

That seemed to appeal to the girls, and so they set off to explore. Bridget had the book she was reading, and Cassie grabbed her sketchbook and some pencils. Laura took one of the sun hats from a hook by the back door, and they wandered across the field to the top of the hill.

The ocean was a dazzling blue gem with the sun bouncing across the waves as they crashed against the shoreline. Laura marveled at how beautiful the panorama was. She found a nice spot to sit on the ground and indicated to the girls they should do the same.

"Cassie, why don't you take out your pencils and draw a nice picture of the ocean and the shore? And, Bridget, come sit by me and we'll work on your reading."

"I can read very well," Bridget whined.

"But the practice can't hurt, can it? Isn't this a nice way to do your lessons? Nothing says you have to be cooped up indoors to study."

Bridget quietly proceeded with her reading with an occasional prompt from Laura, while Cassie toiled vigorously on whatever she was drawing. For Laura, the afternoon was a perfect combination of studies and recess. The sun felt warm on her face, and the rhythm of the ocean's ebb and flow was mesmerizing. Soon, Laura felt as if she could easily fall asleep, so she decided it was time to go in and let the girls have their afternoon siesta. She was certain she, too, could use a little rest.

"Are you girls ready to go back to the house?"

"Just a minute more. I'm not quite finished with my drawing."

"That's fine, Cassie. How much do you have yet to finish?"

"Not much. You and Bridget can go ahead, and I'll catch up in just a bit."

"Well, we'll walk slowly, but don't take too long. Consuela will have my head if you are late for your nap…er, I mean, siesta.

Laura took Bridget's hand, and they began to slowly walk back toward the house. Before they had gone very far, Cassie came running to catch up with them.

"Did you enjoy your outing?" Consuela asked when they entered the kitchen.

"It was a lot of fun," Bridget exclaimed. "We did our studies outside. Can you believe that?"

"And I got to draw the ocean!"

"Can I see your drawing?" Consuela asked.

"Yes, we would all like to see your drawing, Cassie," Laura said.

"Well, I don't know if it is good enough to show everybody. I'm still learning."

Laura was amazed when she took a look at Cassie's sketchbook. Her drawing was alarmingly accurate for someone so young. The detail she had put into a pencil drawing showed a talent well beyond her years.

"That is absolutely marvelous, Cassie," Laura said. "I think we should frame it and hang it in the parlor."

"Do you really think so?" Cassie beamed. "But what if Reuben tries to ruin it?"

"Perhaps we should get Reuben to build a frame for it. Then he would be destroying his own work if he tried to harm it."

"I don't know…" Cassie hesitated.

"For now, let's just put it in a safe place and worry about what to do with it later. It's time you girls get to your room and lie down for a while."

As Consuela led Bridget and Cassie to the room they shared, Dylan rode up and tied his horse to the porch rail. He beat his hat against his leg to get rid of some of the dust. Holding it in his hand, he entered the kitchen and slightly bowed to Laura.

"What brings you here today?" asked Laura.

"I was just on my way back to the rancho and thought I'd stop in to see how everyone was doing." Dylan followed her in as though he belonged there and took a seat at the kitchen table.

"What do you think you are doing?" Laura asked. *The nerve of the man*, she thought.

"I had a little free time and thought perhaps you could offer me a cold lemonade and we could get to know each other a little better."

"What makes you think I want to know you better? And I don't know when Consuela will be back, so I can't offer you any lemonade. This is her kitchen, and I won't intrude on her territory."

"Do you think you could spare a cold glass of water? It's been a hot, dusty day. I've been out looking for stray cattle, and I'm parched."

Laura went to the sink and filled a glass with water, which she placed on the table for him. She turned to leave the kitchen, but Dylan grabbed her arm to stop her.

"Just what do you think you are doing? You are the rudest man I've ever met."

"I just want to sit and chat for a few minutes. Is that being rude, or are you the rude one for running away? Haven't you ever had a friendly chat with a man before?"

"Certainly not with one who had no manners. What can you possibly want to talk to me about? I've only been here a few days and know very little about anything that goes on here."

"What about before you came here? Where did you live, what did you do, why are you here now?"

"I don't see that is any of your business. As to why I'm here, it should be obvious. I have been hired to teach the children, something that appears to be very needed. Especially for Reuben."

"What do you mean about Reuben?"

Fearing she had already said too much, Laura merely said, "He seems to be in need of some discipline, but I don't feel comfortable talking to you about this."

"I am well aware of the problems with Reuben, so don't feel as though you have revealed any family secrets. I just wanted to get to know you a little better, but I can see you are not inclined to be friendly yet so I'll leave you to whatever it is you feel is so important right now."

"I think that is best," Laura said and walked out of the kitchen to head for the solarium to set up for more lessons.

With a wry smile on his face, Dylan finished his glass of water, plopped his hat on his head, and went out the back door. *Yes*, he thought, stroking his mustache, *that little filly is going to take some work.* But he felt up to the task.

Chapter 6

THOUGH FALL WAS WELL on its way, the countryside was experiencing an extremely hot spell. Laura realized she would not be experiencing the beautiful fall colors she had known back home, but she was surprised by how hot it was. Consuela explained to her that they often experienced these hot spells when the wind changed direction and came from the desert instead of the ocean. This phenomenon was called the Santa Ana winds and could occur any time of the year.

"One year, I was trying to roast a turkey for Thanksgiving, and the temperature was 110 outside. We had to eat our Thanksgiving dinner on the veranda because the house was too hot for comfort."

"Wasn't it still hot outside?" Laura asked.

"Yes, but there was still a breeze, even if it was hot. It will take you some time, but you will get used to our heat."

"I don't know," Laura said. "The wintry cold back east was unbearable, but this much heat could be just as bad."

"At least the Santa Ana winds only blow for a few days and then we return to the pleasant ocean breezes. Why don't you take a glass of lemonade and sit on the veranda?"

Laura gladly accepted the lemonade and went to find a shady spot on the porch. She was trying to enjoy having a day off. Manuel had taken the children and their grandmother into town to pick up some supplies, giving Laura a chance to plan the curriculum for the next few weeks. However, she found the heat so oppressive she had not been able to concentrate.

With fall came the harvest of the walnuts, and she knew everyone would be involved in that. She had been told that large canvases were spread out beneath the trees, and the nuts were shaken down. This was done by hand. Then grandmothers, children, and everyone filled cans with nuts picked from the smooth ground. Once the nuts were gathered, they were spread out and dried in three-foot-by-six-foot trays arranged on racks.

Suddenly her thoughts were interrupted by the sound of an approaching horse. *Oh no*, thought Laura, *it's that rude cowboy again. I wonder what he wants.*

Dylan tied his horse to a rail of the stairs and bounded up to sit beside Laura, who was visibly uncomfortable with his closeness. "Man, it's hot enough to wither a fence post today. Say, that lemonade sure looks mighty tasty."

"You'll have to go ask Consuela about that." The chill in Laura's voice could have cooled the entire veranda.

"Not feeling like a hostess today?" Dylan smiled. "Guess I will go see whether Consuela can spare a glass."

Dylan rose and knocked on the back door. When Consuela opened the door, she already had a glass of lemonade to hand him.

"Consuela, you are a doll. Are you sure you won't run away with me?"

"Oh, Senor Dylan, I bet you say that to all the ladies."

"Nope! Just the ones who take care of me like you do." Dylan took the lemonade and went back to sit by Laura, who turned away from him.

"How do you like living here and working with the children?" Dylan was determined to get a conversation going with her.

"Most of the time, I enjoy my job, and the children are delightful...even Reuben."

"Only most of the time?"

"Well, I can't say I enjoy this heat so much. I'm used to a much cooler climate."

"So why did you take a job clear across the country where the climate is so different?"

"Are you writing my biography, Mr. Laughlin? You certainly have a lot of questions."

"Call me Dylan, please! Guess I've always had an inquisitive nature."

"If you must know, my doctor recommended a warmer climate for my health. I just didn't know it would be this much warmer, but I must admit my health issues seem to be improving since I arrived."

"Since I'm not writing your biography, I won't ask what kind of health issues. However, I am glad to hear that you are feeling better and that you are likely to be staying for a while."

Laura did not fully understand why it was so easy to chat with this virtual stranger, and though she fought the idea, she realized she enjoyed his down-to-earth manner.

"As long as we're holding an informal inquiry, how about I ask you some questions? How long have you been working as a vaquero? Is that the right word?"

"It's the Spanish word for cowboy, and I've pretty much been a cowboy all my life. I've only been working on the Valencia ranchero for about a year."

"Where did you work before that?"

"Oh, here and there. Never have stayed too long anywhere. Guess it's the gypsy in me."

Laura wondered just what "here and there" meant. She couldn't help thinking he sounded like a drifter, someone who couldn't really be trusted, yet at the same time, she felt comfortable with him. It had her head spinning trying to figure out just who Dylan Laughlin really was and whether she could or should trust him.

"Well, I better get back to work now that my lemonade is gone and the inquisition is over." Dylan rose and started for the back door to return his glass.

"Who said the inquisition is over?" Laura mused. "I have a lot more questions."

"Guess they'll just have to wait for another time. Besides, here comes Manuel and the family, so I gotta go."

There was mass confusion and disorder as the children disembarked the wagon. Both girls chattered at the same time trying to tell Laura what they had done and about all the things that had been bought. Fiona gathered her bundles and headed to her cottage, leaving Manuel and Reuben to unload the remainder of the supplies and put them away. Laura couldn't help but notice how Reuben had offered to help without being ordered to do so or putting up a big fuss. He seemed to be much more agreeable when his father was not around.

Once the supplies had been stored and Bridget had shown Laura the doll she got in town and Cassie had proudly displayed the paint set her grandmother got for her, they both went to their room to lie down. Laura was about to head to her room to rest a bit when Reuben approached her and asked if she would like to see his invention. Stunned that he was so willing to share his creation with her, she eagerly followed him to the drying sheds. There, he picked up a long pole with a hook attached to one end.

"What is it?" Laura was puzzled.

"It's a shaker…for getting walnuts from the big tall trees that can't be shaken. With this pole, you can reach the walnuts that otherwise can't be reached."

"Reuben, that's such a clever invention. Have you shown this to your father? I'm sure he will be very pleased you created this."

Reuben hung his head as he shook it back and forth. "He'll just hate it and say it is not worth his time."

"You don't know that, Reuben. I believe he will think it is a genius idea."

"He doesn't think anything I do is good enough."

"Let me talk to him. He needs to understand how this can help him with the upcoming harvest."

"Maybe if we just show him how it works, you won't need to say anything. I don't want you to get into trouble either."

"All right. We'll just let a demonstration speak for us both." Laura hesitated and then asked, "Reuben do you think you could make a frame for one of Cassie's drawings?"

Reuben instinctively began to protest. But suddenly, with a shy smile, he said, "You know, I think I probably could, but I would need to know the measurements of the drawing."

"I can get those for you tomorrow," Laura said, realizing that Reuben was anxious to do something constructive instead of destructive. Maybe there was hope yet.

Chapter 7

AS CONSUELA HAD PREDICTED, the scorching Santa Ana winds died down after a few days, and Laura's energy and mood improved. She had taken the measurements of Cassie's drawing and given them to Reuben, who seemed eager to get started on his project. She just crossed her fingers that this experiment would work out the way she planned.

Schoolwork and classes came to an abrupt halt as everyone pitched in to harvest the walnuts and get them on the drying racks. With aching backs and fingers stained black from the walnut husks, everyone fell wearily into bed each night. Laura wondered if she would ever be rested enough to teach again. Worst of all were the black stains on her hands that seemed would never go away.

Reuben's invention of the walnut shaker was used by one of the Mexicans and seemed to work quite well. At first, Ian was skeptical of anything Reuben had devised; but as they had imagined, once he saw how well it worked, he seemed quite pleased.

"Nice work, Reuben," Ian said finally. "Your invention has allowed us to harvest walnuts that probably would have rotted on the tree."

"Miss Laura dared me to make an invention. Then I heard the Mexicans complaining about how hard it was to get the walnuts from the trees that were too big to shake, and so I found a long pole and put a hook on the end of it." Reuben was bursting with pride.

"Perhaps we should thank Miss Laura for daring you to do something useful."

Reuben's disappointment was obvious. Laura began to speak up in his defense, but Ian turned and began giving directions to the workers once again. Laura gave an encouraging nod to Reuben, who did not appear to acknowledge her.

Later that evening, Laura determined to speak to Ian about Reuben when suddenly, Ian asked her to join him in his office.

"Sir, I think…," Laura began.

"Yes, Miss Palmer, I just want to applaud your efforts with the children. They seem to respond favorably to your tutelage, even Reuben."

"Well, sir, I think that they just need a little attention and guidance to help them do the things they like to do anyway. And about Reuben—"

"Never mind about Reuben. He will always manage to do something to disappoint you."

"But, sir, I think if you gave him just a small bit of encouragement, he would surprise you."

"Reuben will definitely surprise me and has several times already, but not in a pleasant manner."

"I really think Reuben is very creative and intelligent and just needs some encouragement to put those abilities to good use."

"Very well, Miss Palmer, you are more than welcome to give it a try. But I warn you, do not be disappointed when your efforts fail." With that, Ian indicated she was free to go, and frankly, Laura was eager to leave before she said something that might surely get her fired.

The next day was filled with excitement because Fiona announced she was taking the family, including Laura, to the San Juan Hot Springs to soak away their sore muscles after the walnut harvest. Laura had heard of the famous hot springs from her doctor back east and was eager to see if soaking in the 120-degree mineral water would cure all her ills as he had claimed.

It would take approximately four to five hours to get to the hot springs; therefore, much preparation needed to be done today so they could depart very early in the morning. It would be an all-day outing, so they would need to pack food for dinner and probably supper as well. Consuela was busy preparing food for the trip while Fiona busied herself with packing bathing costumes, towels, and sundry items for herself and the children. She also gave Laura advice on what she would need to bring along besides her bathing costume.

Laura also decided to pack some lessons for the girls and Reuben to occupy themselves with when they weren't in the water. Bridget needed to practice her numbers, and Reuben needed to be reading more. She was certain Cassie would bring along her sketchbook and pencils, but she also included a book for her to read if she was tired of drawing. When she had finished packing, she went downstairs to help Consuela with the food.

"I was surprised to hear that Mr. Castle will not be joining the family at the hot springs," Laura said as she wrapped some sandwiches Consuela had just finished making.

"He is still very caught up with the drying of the walnuts and preparing them for shipping later. I am just surprised he is letting Manuel drive us there in the wagon. I was afraid he would need him to stay and help too."

Just then, Fiona came into the kitchen. "My son works too many long, hard hours, and he could really use a day at the hot springs. But he insists he must stay and finish the work."

"Is it true the hot springs can cure everything from rheumatism, skin disease, indigestion, and even violent temper?"

"My dear, I think you have been listening to too many rumors and folktales. However, it can be very relaxing and helpful in curing any number of chronic ailments. Drinking the water, too, will work almost a miracle."

"Do you and the family go to the hot springs often?"

"Not as often as we should probably, but it is a tradition to visit the resort after the walnut harvest each year." With that, she went out the back door and headed to her cottage.

"I was just thinking that if the mineral water could cure violent temper, they should be taking Reuben there on a regular basis. Maybe that would fix his temper problems." Laura smiled.

"If that was actually true, then Reuben should be cured by now. No, I think it will take more than mineral water to fix Reuben." Consuela shook her head in despair.

"Well, I plan to see if I can figure out that something extra because I don't think Reuben is as bad as everyone claims."

"Buena suerte," Consuela mumbled. "Good luck."

*****

The family headed out early the next morning. Manuel and Consuela rode in the light delivery wagon with the picnic supplies and other items that were loaded on the back. Following close behind them was Fiona, Reuben, Laura, and the girls in the two-seat spring wagon. Fiona took the reins with Reuben beside her. Laura sat in the back with Bridget and Cassie.

"Let me drive," Reuben begged his grandmother.

"Not just yet, boy. Wait until we have passed through town. You can take the reins on the road out to the hot springs.

Reuben sulked but did as his grandmother asked without further argument. Laura could tell that Fiona had a way of handling Reuben that did not result in confrontation, further proving to her that Reuben's problems stemmed from the treatment by his father.

As they passed the ruins of the mission, Laura asked, "Do the swallows return here every year as I've heard?"

"Yes, the swallows have probably been returning to this area for centuries. The celebration began centuries ago when mission padres observed that the birds returned each year on or about St. Joseph's Day on the church calendar, March 19. Thousands of them fly in to reclaim their old nests in the ancient arches and walls of the mission and to raise their young in the valley," explained Fiona.

"So when do they leave?"

"Every year around the Day of San Juan, October 23. The swallows swirl into the sky and head back to their wintering grounds in Argentina, six thousand miles south."

"That is truly amazing!"

Chapter 8

WHEN THEY REACHED THE hot springs, Reuben pulled the wagon to a halt near some cabins where they could change into their bathing costumes. With Fiona leading the way, they walked down some steps into one of the settling pools where they basked in the warm mineral water. Laura could feel her sore muscles begin to relax, and the aches she had sustained during the walnut harvest seemed to miraculously drift away.

"Some folks believe the hills behind the springs are haunted by the spirits of Indians who died there," Reuben announced proudly.

"Reuben, stop trying to frighten your sisters with tall tales such as that," Laura scolded.

"It is quite true that many folks will not venture farther than the settling pools because of that superstition," Fiona explained.

Laura was not entirely convinced but decided to change the subject. "There are so many folks here," she observed.

"Not nearly as many as would have been here during the summer," Fiona said. "Since the opening of the railroad, the hot springs have become a convenient place to vacation."

"Yeah, they pitch tents or rent rooms at the boarding houses for $5 or $6 a week," Reuben added.

"Capistrano is seeing a lot of changes. It has evolved from a quiet, out-of-way place to a busy, prosperous destination folks return to. The hot springs is largely responsible for the changes," offered Fiona.

After a while, Fiona announced it was time to get out of the pool for a while. As it was, Laura felt she could barely walk as she exited the pool. It really couldn't be a good idea to stay in that hot water for too long for fear of dehydration, she thought, and went to the wagon for some water.

Manuel had spread blankets in the shade of a large eucalyptus tree, and Consuela had set out the picnic lunch. Everyone gathered in the welcome shade and ate lunch. When the children finished eating, they engaged in a game of tag and were soon joined by other children who were visiting the hot springs. At one point, Laura noticed that Bridget was no longer wearing her sunbonnet. Fearing that she would get severely sunburned, Laura went in search of the hat, which she found in some weeds Bridget had fallen in while being chased by Reuben.

"Bridget, come get your sunbonnet before you turn red as a cooked lobster."

"What's a lobster?"

"Lobsters are a kind of sea creature whose shell turns red when it is cooked. The meat inside is very tasty."

"Yuck! I don't want to eat something that has a hard shell."

Laura laughed. "You eat eggs, don't you?" She wondered if the child had never been introduced to clams or shrimp. There was an ocean nearby, after all.

Once the picnic things had been put away and the children had tired of their game of tag, Consuela spread a couple of blankets on the back of the delivery wagon so Bridget and Cassie could take their nap. With the girls asleep and Reuben involved in a game of marbles with some boys his age, Laura and Fiona returned to the settling pool for some additional soaking.

"Reuben seems to be on his best behavior today," Laura said.

"He's not at all as troublesome as his father seems to think."

"He does seem to respond well to you. Why do you think he cannot get along with his father?"

Fiona looked peeved. "That is rather an impertinent question."

"Possibly, but I feel the more I know about what affects the children, especially Reuben, the more it will benefit my ability to tutor them."

"Yes, I can see your point. Although I'm not accustomed to sharing family business, I suppose you should be made aware of the conflict between Reuben and his father."

"I'm not trying to pry, but it would certainly be helpful."

"Maria was married before Ian met her, but her husband got mixed up with some bad hombres, as the Mexicans would say, and was killed shortly after Reuben was born. Maria was struggling to get by after her husband was killed. Ian was staying with friends in San Diego, and that was when he met Maria. I think Ian was charmed by her beauty, as well as feeling sorry for her situation, and so he asked her to marry him. He brought Maria and Reuben here to Walnut Hill to give them a stable home and to fill his big empty house."

"So Reuben is not Ian's biological son. That explains a lot, I think."

"They got along fine until Maria's untimely death."

"My goodness. Do you think their feud has something to do with Maria not being around to mitigate their differences?"

"Possibly. It is believed that the men who killed Reuben's father are also responsible for Maria's death. They apparently were looking for something that her husband had taken from them and thought that she had it."

"How awful that must have been for both Ian and Reuben."

Just then, Laura looked over to where the boys were playing marbles and noticed that Reuben was no longer playing. She looked around the campground but could not see him anywhere. Quickly, she got out of the pool. "Where is Reuben? I don't see him."

"He can't have gone far," Fiona said as she exited the pool as well. "Unless he decided to go back home by walking or running. He does like to take off suddenly for no apparent reason."

"Maybe we should ask Manuel to look around the campground to see if he is still here."

Before a formal search could be initiated, Manuel came around the corner of one of the cabanas with Reuben beside him.

"Look who I found over where the medium was holding an open-air séance."

"I just wanted to see if she could contact my mother so I could ask her why she had to die."

Laura's heart ached by what the boy said, but she said nothing for fear she would break down crying. Fiona calmly hugged the boy and said, "Come on then. Let's wake your sisters and start packing for the journey home. You can drive if you want to, Reuben."

The ride home seemed long and arduous. Everyone was tired from the day's activities, and although the girls had napped, they were both showing signs of sunburn which kept them unusually quiet.

"Reuben, when we get home, I want you to go out to the storeroom and bring me some tallow. It will help soothe Bridget and Cassie's sunburn."

"I will be happy to do that, Miss Laura, right after we unload the wagons and put them away."

"Thank you, Reuben. You are so helpful." Laura felt an occasional compliment could go a long way toward getting through to him.

As tired as everyone was, they made short work of unloading the wagons, putting things away, and having a bite to eat. As soon as the meal was over, Reuben grabbed a candle and headed for the storeroom to retrieve the tallow for Laura.

"Where does he think he's going?" Ian asked as he stood to follow him.

Laura placed her hand on his sleeve. "He has gone to the storeroom to fetch some tallow for me."

Ian sat back down but obviously was not pleased. "He could at least have excused himself properly."

Reuben carried the candle into the storeroom, set it down, and began amusing himself with killing bats. While he was thusly preoccupied, he upset the candle, setting fire to the supplies. Quickly, he grabbed the tallow and ran to the house to get help. Breathlessly, he tried to explain the accident and about the fire. Ian jumped up, signaled Manuel to get some of the hands to help put out the fire, and ordered Reuben to follow him. "You're going to help put out this fire, young man."

Laura started to protest that it was just an accident, but Ian was already out the door. A subtle shake of Fiona's head warned her off.

"I was just going to see if I could help."

"The men will handle what needs to be done."

Since there was no fire department yet in the valley, Ian, Manuel, and Reuben formed a bucket brigade along with some of the Mexican workers, bailing water from the stream that ran alongside the walnut grove. It was slow and arduous work; and Reuben, feeling guilty about what happened, worked as hard as anyone to put out the fire.

Meanwhile, Laura busied herself rubbing tallow on first Bridget and then Cassie.

"That stuff is icky," complained Bridget.

"Maybe, but you will thank me tomorrow when your sunburn doesn't hurt anymore. Now, let's get you two into bed."

It took several hours before the fire was completely contained. Many of the supplies for the household had been destroyed, but the fire did not reach the drying sheds where the walnut crop was laid out. Fiona had returned to her cottage, and only Laura and Consuela sat together at the kitchen table. The tension between father and son was palpable as they came into the house. As soon as she saw the looks on their faces, Laura worried that a fierce clash was about to erupt. Instead, Ian wearily motioned for Reuben to go wash up and get to bed, which he did without further comment.

"Would you like some coffee, Senor Ian?"

"No, Consuela, thank you. I think I'll get cleaned up myself and head off to bed. Tomorrow, we will have to make a list of supplies that will need to be replaced. Tonight, I am too exhausted to think about it." With that, he headed upstairs, leaving Laura, Consuela, and Manuel wondering what would happen next and just how much trouble Reuben was in.

Chapter 9

DESPITE HER EXHAUSTION FROM the day's activities, Laura had trouble falling asleep. She blamed herself for what had happened. If she hadn't asked Reuben to bring her the tallow, then he wouldn't be blamed for accidentally starting the fire that destroyed so many of the household supplies.

For several hours, she contemplated what might happen to Reuben and what, if anything, she could or should do about it. Finally, she decided her best plan of action would be to get the children back on track with their studies and speak to Mr. Castle in Reuben's defense if the need should arise.

The following morning, the family left to attend church in the village. Since Laura was not Catholic, she decided to go for a walk to the hillside overlooking the ocean and explore what might be beyond the hill. As she stood looking at the ocean, she heard the sound of horses' hooves. She turned to see a rider headed in her direction. As he came nearer, she realized it was Dylan Laughlin and wished there was somewhere to go to avoid an encounter with him.

"Good morning, Laura," Dylan waved. "Taking in our breathtaking views?"

"I find it particularly quiet and comforting here overlooking the water. At least I was enjoying it until my solitude was interrupted."

"Ouch!" Dylan declared as he dismounted. "Guess I've been put in my place in no uncertain terms."

"Somehow, you make it impossible to do anything but be rude."

"Well, I'm sorry you feel that way. I saw you standing here and thought you might like to ride with me down to the beach."

"And why, pray tell, would I want to do something like that?"

"Being new to the area and not familiar with how to get around, I just thought I could show you some of the places you have not had a chance to investigate on your own."

"That is very thoughtful of you, but I assure you I have no intention of getting on that horse with you, even if it is to go to the shore."

"Don't you ride?'

"No, Mr. Laughlin, I do not."

"How many times have I told you to call me Dylan. It looks like I need to give you some riding lessons so that you can get around a little better."

"I have no desire to climb onto the back of one of those beasts and be jostled to and fro like some carnival monkey."

"With proper lessons, you would not be jostled, as you put it. Are you afraid of horses? You needn't be. They can be quite gentle and helpful in so many ways."

"Be that as it may, I am not in the market for riding lessons from you or anyone else."

"Fine. Have it your way. But sooner or later, you will need to know how to ride." Dylan said as he climbed back onto his horse. "Heard you folks had some excitement last night. Is everything okay?"

"There was a fire in the storage shed and some supplies were lost, but the men managed to contain it before it reached the drying sheds and no one was injured."

"Do they know how the fire started?"

"I sent Reuben to the shed to fetch some tallow that I could use to soothe our sunburns, and he accidentally knocked over his candle and the fire got out of hand." Laura's voice cracked and tears burned her eyes. "I never should have sent him out there. It's all my fault."

Dylan got off his horse to comfort her. "You can't blame yourself. You didn't knock over the candle."

"But if I hadn't sent him out there, he would not be in so much trouble. I can't imagine what Mr. Castle is going to do to him." Laura wiped her face with the sleeve of her dress. "I'm sorry. I need to get back to the house."

Laura turned and walked defiantly toward the house, leaving Dylan wondering if there was some relationship between Laura and Ian that he did not know about. *That is one strong-willed young woman,* he thought. *But she is not as strong as she tries to convince herself she is. And I wonder what Ian thinks of her.*

In her haste to get away from Dylan and to hide her emotional breakdown, Laura did not notice the small indentation in the path. Her ankle twisted as she went down, and she let out a cry of pain before she could stop herself. As she struggled to get up, Dylan came racing to where she sat on the ground.

"Are you all right?"

"I'll be just fine as soon as I can stand. There's no need for you to bother."

"At least you can allow me to give you a hand so that you can get up." Dylan held out his hand in an attempt to help her up. As she tried to stand, Laura felt another wave of pain and would have landed unceremoniously back on the ground had Dylan not been there to catch her.

"I don't think you are going to be doing any walking on that ankle today," Dylan said. He then turned toward where his horse stood and give a sharp whistle. A look of panic came over Laura's face as she watched the horse draw nearer.

"You don't expect me to get on that thing, do you?"

"Well, you certainly can't walk to the house, and I am most assuredly not going to carry you, though the thought does have some merit." Dylan patiently helped Laura put her good foot in the stirrup and helped her into the saddle. Before she could protest any more, he hopped up behind her and urged the horse toward the house in a gentle walk. Once they reached the back veranda, Dylan hopped down and gently lifted Laura from the saddle and carried her to one of the chairs there.

"Now that wasn't so bad, was it?"

Laura could scarcely speak. She felt flustered and somewhat faint. *It must just be my embarrassment and the effects of the fall,* she thought. However, she was very much aware of the man both as he rode behind her on the horse and as he stood before her now.

"I guess I'm just a bit shaky after my fall," she offered. "Perhaps you could fetch me a glass of water from the kitchen."

"Sure thing. Be right back."

Laura tried to compose herself. After all, being on the horse had not been as frightening as she had imagined, and she couldn't help thinking how nice it had felt to have Dylan's strong arms encircling her as he guided the horse. Why was she having these strange fluttery sensations, especially about a man she truly detested? At that moment Dylan reappeared with a glass of water and a cloth filled with ice.

"Here, drink this and then you need to remove your shoe so that we can put this cold compress on your ankle to keep it from swelling."

Laura's face blushed pink as he lifted the edge of her skirt and began unbuttoning her high-top shoe. But he had placed the compress against her ankle and wrapped it to hold it in place before she could tell him to stop. Dylan stifled a slight grin as he became aware of her discomfort.

"That should hold you until the family returns and they can care for you. Just prop your foot up on this stool, and you should be fine." With that, he stood, came around to the side of her chair, and gently kissed her. Before Laura could protest, he leaped on his horse and quickly rode off in the direction of the shore.

Laura sat in stunned silence wondering why this near-stranger had just kissed her. What a strange thing for him to have done. She wanted to be angry but in fact was somewhat moved by the gesture. If she was totally truthful, she had to admit that she had enjoyed the kiss and wondered what it would have been like if she had returned it. Before she could ponder that possibility any further, the family returned from church and clamored around her in curiosity.

"What happened, Miss Laura?" Bridget asked. "Why is your foot up on that stool with ice on it?"

"Are you injured, Miss Palmer? Do you need a doctor?" asked Ian.

"No, no...I'm fine. I merely tripped on a gopher hole while I was out walking and sprained my ankle. Mr. Laughlin happened to be riding by, and he assisted me to the veranda and placed the compress on it."

"Senor Laughlin, eh?" Consuela didn't even try to hide the twinkle in her eye as she noticed the slight blush on Laura's face. "Why don't you let Manuel help you inside and to your room? I'm sure you would like to lie down for a bit after your little adventure."

"Thank you, Consuela. I would like to lie down and keep my foot elevated for a bit."

"I will bring you some lunch in a little while. Nothing fancy, just some finger sandwiches and some tea."

While Manuel got Laura settled in her room and Consuela began preparing lunch for the family, Ian guided Reuben into his study and told the girls to amuse themselves in the parlor until lunch. Reuben was apprehensive as his father took a seat at his rolltop desk. He could only imagine what was in store for him.

*****

"I'm sorry, father...," Reuben began.

Ian held up his hand to stop Reuben from speaking. "It is not enough to just be sorry all the time. You have to understand that your actions have consequences, and the only way I can be sure you learn that is to see to it that you pay for the supplies we lost."

"How am I going to do that, sir? I have no money."

"You will pay for your actions by working off the cost of new supplies. I have spoken with Senor Valencia, and he is willing to let you work off your debt doing chores around the rancho."

"But..."

"No, this is my decision, and you will do as I say. The matter is not open for discussion. Now you may join your sisters in the parlor until lunch."

"Yes, sir." Reuben got up to leave with his head bowed.

"And another thing. When you are not working on the rancho, you are to be confined to this house or your grandmother's cottage. Do you understand?"

"Yes, sir." Reuben left his father's office and went out on the veranda to think about his father's punishment because that's what it was—punishment. What did he know about working on a rancho? Besides, he had heard some of the Mexicans talking about what a harsh taskmaster Senor Valencia was. Great, just great.

After Laura had eaten a couple of the small sandwiches and had some tea, she lay back on her bed and tried to fall asleep. Her thoughts kept returning to Dylan Laughlin and the tender kiss. Her emotions were all over the place. She knew he was a rogue and the kiss probably meant nothing to him, but why had he done it in the first place?

It bothered her that, despite her anger and embarrassment, she had actually enjoyed his kiss. *What is wrong with me?* she thought. A man like that was not to be trusted and should be put in his place. As she tried to figure out just how to handle the situation, she drifted off to sleep. When she woke, she felt as though the entire episode had merely been a dream, but when she tried to stand, her ankle gave way and she realized she had not been dreaming.

Chapter 10

THE NEXT FEW DAYS were a challenge as Laura had to hobble around using a crude crutch that Manuel had made from a downed tree branch. Nevertheless, she continued tutoring the children in their lessons. With Reuben confined to the house when he wasn't working on the rancho, she was learning just how smart he was in certain subjects.

"You seem to be very advanced in your mathematics, Reuben. Did you attend the local school for a while before I came?"

"No. Father did not want us to go to that school. Mother showed me how to work with numbers and how to read."

"I must say she did an excellent job. What other subjects interest you?"

"I like to learn how things work, how they are put together. Stuff like that."

Laura wasn't quite sure what to do with that information. However, she felt it was important to figure out some way to keep him interested in learning. She was sure Reuben could excel at something if she could just find out what it was.

"How are you coming along with making the frame for Cassie's picture of the ocean?"

"I haven't really had a chance to do anything with it yet since I'm confined to the house or working for Senor Valencia."

"Let me talk to your father to see if he will allow you some time to find some wood for your project. Maybe you could spend class time putting it together."

"I don't think he will let me anywhere near the tools and wood I would need. He thinks I'm a menace who will destroy everything."

"Perhaps you could see if Senor Valencia has the supplies you need."

"I don't know..." Reuben hesitated. "Maybe Dylan could help me get what I need. I see him nearly every day that I'm at the rancho."

"What kind of work do you do on the rancho?" Laura asked, wanting to steer the conversation away from Dylan.

"Mostly, I have to clean the barn, make sure the water troughs are full so the horses can drink, and once in a while, I get to ride out with Dylan to check on the cattle."

Suddenly, Laura had a vision of being in the saddle of Dylan's horse and how she thought she would be frightened but wasn't. Maybe she should learn to ride.

"How long have you been riding horses, Reuben?"

"I don't know. Seems like I've always known how to ride. Even the girls learned to ride when they were just little. Do you know how to ride?"

"No, I'm afraid I never had the opportunity to be around horses. They kind of frighten me, but I think I would like to know how to ride."

"I bet Dylan would be glad to teach you. They have several gentle horses on the rancho that would be great for you to start with."

"I'll have to think about that, Reuben." Laura just bet Dylan would be more than happy to get her on a horse, but what then?

Bridget and Cassie were finishing their lessons for the day, so all three children went out on the veranda, with Laura hobbling along behind them.

"I'll just sit here and watch you play for a while. What games do you like to play? Tag? Hide-and-go-seek?"

"Hide-and-go-seek!" squealed Bridget, jumping from one foot to another. "Let's play hide-and-go-seek. Reuben, you're it. Cassie and I will hide, and you have to find us."

As Laura watched the children enjoy their game, she thought about what Reuben had said about his father thinking he was a menace. He was rambunctious sometimes, sure, but he was so watchful and protective of his sisters. She was contemplating approaching Ian again when he appeared around the side of the house looking like a storm cloud about to burst.

"What is going on here? Reuben, I told you to stay in the house when you were not working!"

"The children are just having a sort of recess. They have been studying hard today and need to let off a little steam. I didn't think it would hurt anything if Reuben stayed in the yard where I could see him."

"I just heard one of the girls saying she could not find him. I thought perhaps he had taken off again."

"They were just having a friendly game of hide-and-go-seek. It was Reuben's turn to hide, that's all."

"Well, all right then. But you make sure Reuben stays within the boundaries of the house."

"Of course, sir. Could I ask you a favor? Is it possible for Reuben to have access to some wood and a few tools? He wants to build a frame for one of Cassie's pictures."

Ian thought for a moment, then said, "I guess that would be fine, but only if Manuel goes with him to get what he needs. I don't need him setting fire to anything else. What makes him think he can make a picture frame, anyway?"

"Sir, I asked him to do it, and I think we should at least give him the chance to try."

With a disgusted shake of his head, Ian turned and went back to the drying sheds. Laura wished she could understand what made that man so hostile at times. Well, she would just concentrate on doing her very best with the children, and hopefully, he would see that his mood was very disruptive to their lives, not just Reuben's.

Within a few days, Laura was able to get around without the aid of the crutch, although she still had a slight limp. The days seemed to pass relatively smoothly with little or no conflict or major dramas. Reuben seemed to actually enjoy his "punishment" at the rancho. Laura suspected it was due in large part to time spent with Dylan.

Reuben had confided in her that Dylan was taking him along when he went to check on the cattle. Despite her misgivings about

Dylan, he did seem to take an interest in Reuben and was trying to teach him valuable lessons that could not be learned in the classroom.

*****

On one particularly gloomy day, when Reuben was not working at the rancho, he brought Laura the frame he had made for Cassie's drawing and asked if it was what she wanted.

"This is exactly what I was looking for!" exclaimed Laura. "I never expected it to be this well done. Reuben, it's magnificent."

"Dylan helped me with the corners. He said they needed to be mi…mi…"

"You mean 'mitered'?"

"That's it…mitered. He said it would look better that way and last longer."

"Well, he is exactly right about that. Let's get Cassie's drawing and get it framed. Cassie, come look at the frame Reuben made. Isn't it marvelous?"

"Oh, Reuben, you made that for me? Let me go get my picture."

Reuben nodded shyly and gazed at the floor almost as if he couldn't believe they weren't upset with him. As Laura and Cassie placed her drawing on a piece of cardboard and set it into the frame, Reuben began to see that what he had done was truly being appreciated, and a sly smile crossed his face.

"Now, where shall we hang this so that everyone can enjoy it? How about above the fireplace?"

"That would be perfect, Miss Laura," said Cassie.

"Reuben, could you go fetch a nail and hammer so we can put this picture up?"

"Are you sure I'm allowed to do that? Manuel isn't here right now to go with me."

"Well, I think you are quite capable of getting what we need, but just so there is no trouble later, I'll go with you. We can get the nail and hammer together, okay?"

With that, Reuben and Laura went out to the storage shed where the tools were kept. On the way, they encountered Ian just coming in from the drying sheds.

"What is going on here?" Ian inquired.

"Reuben and I are going to get a hammer and nail. We were going to hang Cassie's drawing of the ocean over the fireplace. Reuben has made a fine frame for it."

"I don't think the fireplace is the best place to display children's drawings and crude frames."

"Have you even seen the drawing or the frame?" Laura was indignant.

"No, but I do not want my home cluttered with amateur art projects. These things would best be put in the classroom area or in their rooms."

"That is just nonsense. Your son and daughter have created something quite lovely, and I believe it should be displayed openly for all to see."

"I insist on seeing this supposed work of art before I can allow you to hammer a nail in the wall. Then, I will make my judgment on the matter." Ian turned and went back to the drying sheds.

"Well, I never…" Laura turned back to Reuben who was cowering behind her. "Let's get that nail and hammer anyway. Then, we will be ready when he decides it is okay to hang the picture."

"I am so glad you came with me, Miss Laura. I would have really been in trouble. Thanks for standing up for Cassie and me."

"Someone needs to think about you children, and I don't think he understands how his words can hurt."

The foggy gloom continued throughout the day, and so Laura and the children stayed inside. After their lessons were finished, they amused themselves with a rousing game of tiddlywinks which Reuben, of course, won. Cassie's picture was placed on top of the mantle and leaned against the wall. The nail and hammer lay beside it.

Later that evening, after much prodding from the children at the dinner table, Ian promised to take a look at the picture in question. Everyone followed him into the parlor in anticipation of his reaction. Reuben held back from the others in case the verdict was not a favorable one. For quite some time, Ian stood in front of the fireplace, staring up at the picture on the mantel without saying a word. Laura noticed him touch his finger to the corner of his eye as if to stop a tear. She was warmed by the gesture and the thought that maybe he had misjudged his children.

Finally, turning to the children, Ian said, "You may hang the picture above the fireplace. I had no idea you two were so talented." He then left the room while everyone just stood there with mouths open.

Laura helped Reuben determine the right spot for the nail and made sure it was hanging straight. She then put an arm around both Cassie and Reuben to give them a hug. Not to be left out, Bridget snuggled between her brother and sister, "Me too! Me too!"

"Yes, you too, Bridget," Laura said, and they all laughed.

Chapter 11

AS THE HOLIDAY SEASON approached, Laura found herself thinking about her home back in New England. She missed the first dusting of snow, the beginning of pheasant hunting, and the hot chocolate after an afternoon of ice skating. It seemed so strange there had been no leaves changing colors and no cooler temperatures at night resulting in frost on everything the next morning.

To distract herself from feelings of homesickness, Laura began scanning the mail-order catalogs for ideas for gifts to give the children. In addition, she had Bridget and Cassie cut out colored construction paper to create a garland to drape across the mantle. She also showed them how to cut out paper snowflakes to put on the windows. They seemed unsure of what they were supposed to do, but once they began, they made quick work of it.

Reuben looked up from his chalkboard where he had been working on some mathematical problems. "What a bunch of nonsense. Who puts snowflakes on their windows in California?"

"Well, I suppose it does seem a bit strange, but it reminds me of my home in New England where it snows this time of year."

"That's fine, but it just seems odd, that's all." However, Laura noticed him watching Cassie very carefully cut out a snowflake as though he were trying to figure out how to do it.

When not in the classroom with the children, Laura retired to her room in the tower to continue her search for ideas for Christmas gifts for the family. She had decided to give Reuben a copy of

Huckleberry Finn by Mark Twain, and she had found a nice easel for Cassie so she could better use her paints. Bridget was easy; she found a beautiful doll that would be perfect.

While searching for gifts for the children, Laura also discovered some nice gifts for the rest of the family. There was a fancy hair comb for Consuela's beautiful dark hair and a pocketknife with four blades for Manuel. For Fiona, she had discovered a lovely Spanish lace shawl. She had seen a lovely pen set she thought might do for Ian, but she was really quite unsure as to whether she should get anything for him. Did he even need a pen? She would have to ponder that for a while before she knew what she would do.

As the weather cooled some and work on the rancho slowed down a bit, Reuben began spending more time in the classroom with the girls and without complaint. Laura realized that Reuben had real potential for learning and was eager for whatever came next. She also noticed that there were no tantrums nor destructive behavior since she had arrived and couldn't help but wonder what had precipitated the chaos she had encountered when she arrived.

The week before Thanksgiving, Dylan arrived with Reuben when he returned from the rancho. He was leading another horse behind him. Laura looked up from the book she had been reading on the veranda and wondered what he was doing here again.

"This seems the perfect day to begin your riding lessons," Dylan explained.

"I thought I told you in no uncertain terms that I was not going to learn to ride a horse." Laura rose and turned to go into the house.

"If you think you can survive for very long in this part of the country without being able to ride, you are sadly mistaken."

"Come on, Miss Laura, you need to learn to ride," Reuben said. "You are always teaching us new things. Now, it is your turn to learn something new."

"Are you ganging up on me too, Reuben?" Laura laughed but was still very apprehensive. "I suppose it couldn't hurt to try something I have never done before. Won't I need some sort of riding costume?"

"Eventually, we can get you outfitted, but for today, you can come along just as you are." Dylan dismounted, handing the reins for both horses to Reuben. "I've brought along Sophie, a very gentle mare who will do her best to make your first experience a delightful one."

"Just put your hand on the horn and your left boot in the stirrup, then just swing your leg over." She did as he told her even as her heart began to race. Suddenly aware that her skirt had risen above her shoes, she blushed and carefully pulled it down as best she could. Dylan turned to his horse so as not to embarrass her further. As she tried to get comfortable, it occurred to her that the horse beneath her was like a giant muscle ready to flex.

"It's higher than I thought it would be."

"Just touch the reins against her neck, and she'll turn for you like this. To make her go, just tap her sides with your heels. To stop, pull back."

Steeling herself, she fluttered the reins and tapped the horse on the sides. Nothing. She tapped again, but the horse remained as immobile as a statue. Terrified, she tried again. The horse then slowly backed away from the veranda and began to walk toward the trail that led to the hilltop. Dylan quickly rode up on one side of her, while Reuben flanked her on the other side.

"See, Miss Laura. It's not so bad, is it?" Reuben encouraged.

Not wanting to disappoint her pupil nor appear unwilling to learn something new, Laura said, "It does not seem to be as terrifying as I had imagined. I just hope this horse doesn't decide to take off running across the field."

"The horse will only do what you tell it to, so if you don't kick your heels hard into her sides, she will not take off running. Remember, you are the boss. The horse will do what you tell her to."

By the time the horses reached the crest of the hill overlooking the ocean, Laura had begun to feel a bit more at ease. However, she suddenly panicked when she realized she needed to stop the horse or they would both go racing down the other side of the hill.

"How did you say I am supposed to stop this thing?"

"Gently pull back on the reins," Dylan instructed. Laura did, and the horse stood still.

"Now, if you want her to turn around so that you can go back to the house, simply pull gently on the rein that is on the side of the direction you want to turn. Why don't you pull on the right rein and see what happens?"

"Oh my gosh! She's turning to the right. Now what?"

"Just hold the reins like you were before you turned and gently nudge her sides again."

Laura did as he instructed, but when she urged the horse forward, she kicked a little harder than she meant to and the horse took off at a slow trot. Laura began to scream and started slipping off the saddle a little bit. "Help! I'm going to fall off!"

Dylan rode up beside her, righted her in the saddle, and grabbed the reins to slow the horse to a walk. Laura immediately tried to get down off the horse but sadly was not quite sure how to do that without falling and making a bigger fool of herself.

"You're doing great, Laura," Dylan encouraged. "You just tried to skip to lesson three without learning all of one and two."

"I don't think there will be any need for lessons two and three. I simply am not cut out for riding horses."

"Nonsense. You got a little spooked is all. Next time, you'll have a better feel for how much nudging to give the horse."

Laura wasn't so sure, but she did want to give it a try so that Reuben could understand that everyone can do poorly at first, then try something again until they get it right. *How did I get myself into this?* wondered Laura.

When they reached the house, Dylan instructed Laura how to place her foot in the stirrup and bring her other leg over the horse then slide down to the ground. Laura felt self-conscious and awkward doing this, but feeling the ground underfoot felt wonderful, though her legs were a little wobbly at first.

"You may be stiff and sore tomorrow, but a little wintergreen oil should take care of that. I'm sure Consuela has some in the house." Dylan mounted his horse, took Sophie's reins from Reuben, and rode off toward the rancho.

Laura limped into the kitchen and immediately asked Consuela for some wintergreen oil, which she took with her to her room. She already felt sore in places she didn't even realize she had.

Chapter 12

ALTHOUGH THE DAYS WERE often overcast and a gentle breeze blew in from the ocean causing Laura to wear her shawl to go outside, there were still many sunny days that made her question how it could possibly be nearing Thanksgiving. She quickly recovered from the aches she had experienced after her riding lesson, due in large part to Consuela's wintergreen oil. Just when she began to feel normal again, Dylan and Reuben showed up with Sophie to give her another lesson. She felt decidedly more comfortable this time and even nudged the horse into a canter on the way back to the house.

"You seem to be in a rush to get home and off that horse," Dylan said with a laugh.

"I just wanted to see if I could go a bit faster without needing to be rescued this time."

"You done good, Miss Laura," said Reuben.

"*Did well*, Reuben. I did well," Laura corrected.

"Oh right. I forgot!"

"It's all right, Reuben," she remarked when she saw him hang his head a bit. "Guess I can't stop being a teacher, even while out riding."

"I must say you did quite *well* also," Dylan added with an emphasis on the word *well*.

Laura dismounted and was about to go into the house when Dylan suggested that she might benefit from a good soak at the mineral hot springs. As Laura was about to protest, Reuben dismounted and said, "That's a great idea, Miss Laura. We all could use another day at the hot springs."

Laura hoped that all didn't include Dylan but figured he would be busy with work on the rancho, so she nodded in agreement. "I'll check with Mr. Castle to be sure such an outing would be appropriate."

"Do you have to check with him every time you want to do something? Besides, I'm sure he would have no problem with it," commented Dylan.

"He is my employer, and it seems only reasonable that I should seek his opinion before taking the children on an excursion." With that, Laura stomped up the steps of the veranda and into the house.

Dylan looked at Reuben, shrugged his shoulders, shook his head, picked up Sophie's reins, and rode off in the direction of the rancho.

A few days later, the entire family, including Ian, Fiona, Consuela, and Manuel loaded the wagons and headed for the hot springs. The day was sunny and bright, and everyone was in a good mood. Laura was especially warmed to see Ian pleasantly interacting with his children. As they passed the mission ruins, Laura couldn't help wondering why it had never been restored after the earthquake.

Almost as if he had read her mind, Ian suddenly said, "I heard the other day there is a bunch of folks calling themselves the Landmark Group who plan to restore several of the missions in California. San Juan Capistrano is to be their first project."

"Won't that be nice?" said Fiona.

"It will no doubt bring more tourists to the town," Laura said.

"That could be both a good thing and a bad thing," observed Ian. "The local businesses would do well, but with more people comes more chance of outlaws and increased crime."

Well, Laura thought, *leave it to Ian to cast a negative view on something*. She decided right there and then not to let him ruin her day at the hot springs. She was looking forward to soaking out some of those aches she had from horseback riding. Despite the soreness, which was getting less severe each time she rode, she was discovering she enjoyed riding far more than she ever thought she could.

There was something about the power of the animal beneath her, the wind in her hair, and the sun on her face that gave her such a feeling of freedom, a freedom she hadn't even known she was missing. She was shocked to realize she was also enjoying the time spent with Dylan.

As soon as everyone had changed into their bathing costumes, Laura noticed Ian, Fiona, and the girls had all headed for one of the larger pools; so she decided to let them have their family time together and went to find a spot in one of the smaller pools some distance away. She noticed also that Reuben had gone off to shoot marbles with a few of his friends.

Sinking into the soothing warmth of the mineral water, Laura closed her eyes and let the water flow over her aching body. She sensed that someone else had stepped into the pool but was enjoying her reverie too much to pay any attention. It was, after all, a public resort; and while she enjoyed the solitude, she did not expect to be alone forever. She jumped, however, when she heard a familiar voice say, "I see you took my advice."

Opening her eyes, she found herself staring into the crystal-clear blue eyes of Dylan Laughlin. Of all the people she could have shared a pool with, he was the last one she would have chosen. "What are you doing here?"

She felt a blush rising from her throat to her face as she stared at him. His navy bathing costume with green-and-white stripes on the edges of his sleeves and on the bottom of the pants that fell just above his knees gave her a view of his sinewy arms and legs. She could almost feel the strength they held.

"Cowboys get saddle sore too, you know."

"Actually, no. I didn't know. I figured you would be busy chasing cows or whatever it is you do."

"I don't chase cows! I ride herd on the cattle and try to make sure they don't get sick or no one tries to steal them."

"Who's watching them now that you are here?"

"The bulk of the cattle has been sold and shipped to market. The breeding stock is all in the corral at the rancho. That means that I can have a day off now and then, if that meets with your approval."

Laura ignored his sarcastic remark and closed her eyes so she could once again relax in the soothing waters. Perhaps, she thought, he will take the hint and go somewhere else.

"What are you afraid of, Laura?"

Laura's eyes flew open as she stared at him. "I'm not afraid of anything. What gave you that idea?"

"You are very rigid and closed off, except when you are with the children. You are fantastic with them, and I can see a definite improvement in Reuben since you came to Walnut Hill."

"I enjoy working with the children."

"That is very obvious. Do you want to have children of your own someday?"

"I don't see that is any of your business, but yes, I would like to get married and have my own children to raise. I'm still a bit young to be worrying about such things, however."

"Not afraid of becoming a spinster?" A mischievous smile crossed Dylan's face.

"I told you, I'm not afraid of anything." Laura rose and started to leave the pool. Just then, Ian stepped into the pool.

"Is this scoundrel bothering you, Laura?" asked Ian, giving Dylan a hardy slap on the back. "Sit down, Laura. No need to leave just yet."

"I should probably give Fiona a hand with the children."

"Nonsense. Mother loves spoiling my children. Besides, she has Consuela to help her keep an eye on Bridget and Cassie. Heaven only knows what Reuben could be up to."

Laura returned to her spot in the pool and wondered what on earth had prompted Ian to come over. Was he truly concerned for Laura's safety with Dylan? Did he know something she didn't? While she was annoyed by Dylan's manner, she never felt threatened around him. It might be interesting to observe the interaction between the two men. It would definitely give her a better picture of each one's character.

"What brings you out to the springs today, Dylan? I would have thought you would be pretty busy at the rancho."

"As I explained to Laura, the herd has been shipped and the breeding stock is in the corral, so I have no need to be on the range for a while."

Ian turned to Laura. "I understand you are learning to ride."

"Yes. Mr. Laughlin has been kind enough to teach me how to handle a horse."

"How very generous of you, Dylan. I'm not quite sure why you feel Laura needs to know how to ride, but as long as it doesn't take her away from her teaching duties, I guess there is no harm."

"How generous of you, Ian."

Laura couldn't help but notice the edge of sarcasm in Dylan's remark. She watched Ian carefully to see if he was going to respond. She could only hope there would be no bad blood between them. She really didn't want an argument to ensue. To change the subject, Laura said, "I was thinking of giving the children a few days off for Thanksgiving, if you have no objections, Mr. Castle."

"I see no reason a few days off would hurt anything, and please, call me Ian."

"Thank you, Mr.—ah, Ian. The children have been doing so well. They deserve a little break."

"You have done a wonderful job working with the children. I have even noticed a remarkable improvement in Reuben lately."

Finally, thought Laura. "I think Dylan has had as much a hand in that as I have."

"What have you been up to now, Dylan?"

"Nothing out of the ordinary, Ian. You sent him to the ranch to work off his punishment for starting the fire in the supply shed. I've just been in charge of keeping him busy."

"I see," said Ian thoughtfully. "Well, his time at the rancho will be up at the end of this month, so you won't need to concern yourself with keeping him busy anymore."

Laura stood and stepped out of the pool. "I think I need some time in the shade. Don't want to wrinkle like a prune." Laura walked over to where Fiona and Consuela had set up lunch on the back of one of the wagons. Looking back to the pool she had just left, she noticed a rather heated discussion taking place between Ian and

Dylan. Wonder what that's about, she thought as she prepared to enjoy some of Consuela's wonderful food.

As Laura was finishing her lunch, Dylan came over from the pool and asked her if she had seen Reuben. She looked around and said, "The last time I saw him, he was playing marbles with some friends over there. You might check to see if the medium is here. He tends to visit her, I've noticed."

Dylan took off in the direction Laura had indicated she had last seen the boy. Just then, Ian walked up to her and asked what Dylan had said to her.

"He just wanted to know if I had seen Reuben."

"Why would he need to locate Reuben?"

Laura shrugged. "I don't know. He just seemed concerned."

"I guess I'll go see what he is up to. Will you tell Fiona and Consuela to begin gathering our things? We need to be heading home soon."

The women began loading the lunch items into the wagon, then went to change out of their bathing costumes. Laura kept wondering why Dylan was so intent on finding Reuben and whether his concern had anything to do with the heated discussion she had witnessed between the two men. By the time they had everything ready to go, Ian had returned, but there was no sign of Dylan or Reuben.

"I can't believe that boy has run away again." Ian ran his fingers through his hair. "I would have thought a month's worth of punishment would make him change his ways."

"Are you sure he has run away?" Laura asked. "Is it possible he and some friends just went for a hike in the hills or something?"

"He should know better than to take off without at least telling us he was going."

"Maybe he feared you would not let him and, consequently, embarrass him in front of his friends."

Just about that time, Reuben came around the corner of one of the cabins with several other boys about his age or slightly older. Ian rushed over to him and grabbed him by the arm, practically dragging him to the wagons.

"Just where have you been, young man, and what have you been up to?"

Reuben cast a furtive glance back toward the other boys, then looked up to his father and said, "Some of the fellas were showing me a good place for fishing. What is wrong?"

"You just decide to go off on your own without letting any of us know where you are or what you are up to? What were you trying to hide? Have you been drinking?"

"No, sir, I have not been drinking, except some of the mineral water. And I was not trying to hide anything. I just didn't think—"

"That's right! You just didn't think!" Ian was practically shouting and beginning to make a scene. "Get your clothes changed quickly so we can get going."

Laura felt saddened by what she had just seen and heard. She didn't feel it was her place to interfere with a family dispute, but she felt sorry for Reuben and a bit miffed with Ian. She felt he was being far too harsh with the boy for doing what boys do, and she wondered where Dylan had disappeared to.

Chapter 13

PREPARATIONS BEGAN FOR THE huge Thanksgiving feast that would feed not only the Castle family but all the hands and workers that helped with the walnut harvest. Due to the incident at the hot springs, Ian had added an additional two weeks to Reuben's time working at the rancho. Of course, Laura knew Reuben did not mind the additional time. He seemed to actually thrive on the duties he had to perform, and she knew he really liked spending time with Dylan.

With Christmas only a few weeks away, Laura had already placed her order with the mail-order company. With her Christmas shopping done and the children having some time off for the holiday, Laura went down to the kitchen to see if she could lend a hand with some baking. She always enjoyed baking with her aunt and missed the opportunity to get her hands on some dough.

"Miss Laura, what brings you to the kitchen? Did you want something to eat? Lunch will be in about an hour."

"No, Consuela. I came to give you a hand."

"What you mean 'give me a hand'? There is nothing wrong with my hands."

"I want to help with baking. I can make excellent pies, cakes, cookies, and bread. I want to help."

"Ah, but there is no need. Mr. Ian pays me very well to do these things."

"I'm sure he does, and I don't wish to imply that you cannot do it. But I enjoy baking and would like the opportunity to help out, to contribute."

"Oh, you are just looking for something to do since you are not teaching right now!"

"Exactly! What can I help you with?"

"Well, since you put it that way, we can always use lots of cookies during the holidays. Can you make some holiday cookies?"

"You bet I can. Just show me where you keep the supplies and I'll get busy."

Laura began with her aunt's favorite sugar cookie recipe, creating holiday shapes with the cookie cutters she brought with her. The following day, she made gingerbread men with her aunt's famous ginger cookie recipe. Finally, she created a Victorian gingerbread house, which she enlisted the help of Bridget and Cassie to decorate. Bridget seemed to enjoy helping in the kitchen despite not being very adept at decorating cookies, but Cassie excelled using her artistic flair to create lovely designs. Consuela muttered something about the mess in her kitchen, but Laura assured her they would have it cleaned to her standard before they finished.

The Thanksgiving feast overwhelmed Laura who was accustomed only to a modest dinner with her aunt and a few of her aunt's friends. Long tables were set end to end on the side veranda with seating for approximately twenty people. A smaller table was set on the back veranda for the children. Aside from Reuben, Cassie, and Bridget, there were ten or so children belonging to some of the workers' families.

When Laura was about to sit with the children, Consuela took hold of her elbow and led her to the large table where she indicated the chair Laura was to sit in.

"You sit with the adults, not the children."

"But I assumed there would need to be supervision of the children."

"Not today, querida. Enjoy a holiday."

Laura sat where Consuela indicated and nodded greetings to the workers seated near her. Just before Ian began the blessing, Laura became aware of someone sitting in the chair beside her. Her breath caught when she found herself looking once again into the blue eyes of Dylan Laughlin.

"Happy Thanksgiving, Laura," Dylan said, as though it was the most natural thing in the world.

"Happy Thanksgiving." Laura thought it only polite to return the greeting, though she wasn't feeling very happy or thankful at the moment.

"You needn't look so put out, Laura. Ian invited me, as I have no family in the area."

"That was very generous of him. I hope you enjoy your meal," Laura said as she bowed her head in anticipation of whatever blessing was coming. She was not familiar with the Catholic form of grace but planned to honor whatever was said. As soon as the prayer ended and everyone crossed themselves, the food started being passed around with everyone talking at once. With so many accents, it was difficult for Laura to pick out what was being said.

"The Castles always put on a big spread every year, so I hear." Dylan had leaned close so that she could hear him.

Though she didn't care for his closeness, she responded, "They certainly have outdone themselves. I don't know when Consuela had time to prepare all this. I offered to help, but all I did was bake some cookies and a gingerbread house."

"I've been told the wives of the workers contribute, so Consuela didn't have to do it all. Wait a minute…you baked cookies?"

"Don't sound so surprised. I was raised in New England where it is expected that young girls will marry and therefore are trained in the domestic arts."

"And do you plan to marry?"

"Someday, I imagine, though I feel it would be important to find the right man before even considering that possibility."

"Just what would the right man be like?"

"Not that it is any business of yours. But I think the right man would be educated, well-mannered, possess a sense of fair play. I don't know. I think I will just know if I should ever meet such a person."

"What about wealthy and loves children?"

"He should definitely love children, but I'm not so sure wealth is an important factor."

"But you wouldn't turn down a wealthy man if he possessed all these other admirable qualities, would you?"

"This conversation has gone quite far enough. I'm not interested in discussing my personal life with you." Laura turned to the person seated on the other side of her and asked them to pass the mashed potatoes. She managed to ignore Dylan for the remainder of the meal and enjoyed listening to the conversations of the folks seated near her.

The woman seated across the table from her suddenly asked. "Have you encountered the white lady?"

"What do you mean?" inquired Laura. "What white lady?"

"The ghost that is said to haunt this house," the woman explained. "Some say it is the ghost of the late Senora Castle who comes back to watch over her children."

"I'm afraid I don't believe in ghosts, senora." As the conversation continued around her, Laura glanced toward the end of the table where Ian was sitting to see his reaction, but he seemed to be deep in discussion with his foreman that he was not aware of what was happening. Couldn't the man forget about business long enough to enjoy a family feast? It was probably just as well, she thought. No telling what his reaction would be to the subject of his wife's ghost.

"It is simply not true, Laura," Fiona interrupted. "Some have claimed to have seen a presence of light that appears to be a young, beautiful lady with dark hair and a long white dress. But I assure you, we do not have a ghost at Walnut Hill."

"No, it is true," the woman insisted. "She has supposedly walked through the houses of some prominent families in San Juan."

"That's preposterous rumors. Pay no attention to them, Laura." Fiona indicated there was to be no more talk of ghosts. Everyone went back to their meals and conversations.

Laura turned and noticed that Dylan had left the table. She wondered if it had something to do with the talk of a white lady and ghosts. Good riddance as far as she was concerned.

Chapter 14

HOLIDAY PARTIES SEEMED TO abound in Capistrano Valley. Fiona and Ian were both invited to many of the prestigious homes, though not always to the same ones. Laura was invited to join them at the home of Judge Eagan but declined the invitation to the party at the Valencia rancho. She was in no mood to encounter Dylan Laughlin, who most assuredly would make an appearance at the home of his employer.

The items she ordered from the mail-order catalog arrived at the train station a couple of weeks before Christmas. Laura rode into town with Manuel to pick up her packages and to help with the supplies they needed to pick up for the coming holiday celebrations.

"Looks like you bought out the mail-order house, Miss Laura," Manuel said as he lifted her packages onto the back of the wagon.

"Believe me, Manuel, that would not be possible. That catalog is just crammed full of things, not only beautiful things like dresses and hats but useful things like saddles and tools and guns, though I personally abhor guns."

"Sometimes, here in the West, a gun can be a handy companion."

"That may be. But all too often, it seems men prefer to use their guns against each other, and I don't see any good coming from that."

Manuel nodded his agreement and flicked the reins to get the horse to head home with the wagon loaded with Laura's packages and the household supplies. As they approached the big house on the hill, Dylan Laughlin rode up to stop them.

"Isn't Reuben with you?" he asked.

"No. I thought Reuben was working at the rancho today," Laura said, the worry showing quite plainly on her face when she noticed the holster and gun riding on Dylan's hip.

"He did not show up for work today, and everyone just assumed he had gone into town with you two. Now, who knows what that rascal is up to now?"

"Have you checked with Ian, I mean, Mr. Castle?" asked Laura.

"Of course I have." Dylan's impatient tone was not lost on Laura. "Who do you think sent me out to intercept you and to find him? He seems quite sure Reuben has run off again."

"We need to get these supplies and Miss Laura's packages unloaded, then I can saddle a horse and ride out with you to try and find Reuben." Manuel once again flicked the reins and headed to the house. Dylan rode along and helped Manuel unload the supplies. Laura made several trips to carry her purchases to her room.

"I can give you a hand with those, if you like," Dylan said.

"That's quite all right. I prefer to handle these packages myself. Besides, the faster you and Manuel can unload the supplies, the sooner you can get out looking for Reuben." Picking up the remainder of her packages, Laura disappeared into the house without so much as a backward glance. Dylan merely shook his head and muttered something about "danged independent woman."

After Laura had secured her packages in the back of her armoire, she went to Reuben's room to see if she could discover any clues as to where he might have gone or why he had run away again. Much to her surprise, when she opened the door to his room, she found Reuben fast asleep on the top of his coverlet. She gently shook him.

"Are you all right, Reuben? Are you ill?"

"What?" a groggy Reuben stared blankly at her.

"Do you realize everyone is out looking for you? They think you ran away."

Sitting up and rubbing the sleep from his eyes, Reuben said, "I'm fine. I came up here to look for something I wanted to show Dylan. I guess I just laid down and fell asleep. What time is it?"

"I can't believe no one thought to check your room for you. It's nearly dinnertime. When did you come up here?"

"Oh my gosh! I was supposed to go to the rancho today. I'm going to be in so much trouble." Reuben began pacing around his room when he stopped suddenly and reached down to pick up a book that was lying by his bed. "I wanted to show Dylan a picture in this book, and I started reading. That must be what made me fall asleep. What do I do now, Miss Laura? My father is going to skin my hide."

"I think he may be relieved enough that you have not run away that he won't skin your hide, as you say. I need to run down to see if I can catch Manuel and Dylan before they take off to parts unknown to look for you."

"I'll come with you. If my father is here, I want you to be nearby when he finds out I fell asleep instead of doing my chores."

Laura and Reuben were able to catch Manuel and Dylan to let them know it was not necessary to ride off to look for Reuben. As everyone came back into the house, Ian stepped out of his office.

"Where did you find him?" Ian asked, looking at Manuel and Dylan.

"He was asleep in his room," Laura interjected. "Did no one think to check on him there?"

"Why was he sleeping in his room? He was supposed to be doing chores at the rancho." Ian's tone was harsh and accusing.

"I went up to my room to get a book so I could show Dylan a picture that was in it. I started reading a passage, and I guess I just fell asleep."

"That makes no sense. How could you be that tired after sleeping all night?"

"Now wait a minute," Dylan interrupted. "He did say he had a picture of Wyatt Earp he wanted to show me."

"Yeah, and I started reading about the Gunfight at the O.K. Corral, and I guess I just fell asleep."

"Well, all right then," Ian conceded and went back into his office. Laura was still amazed that no one, especially Ian, had bothered to check his room but had instead just assumed the worst of the boy. She put her arm around his shoulders and led him into the parlor to play with the girls until supper.

*****

The days just before Christmas were filled with excitement and anticipation. Laura gave the girls lessons on baking and supervised Reuben who was making a gift for his grandmother out of walnut shells. She also found time during their siestas to wrap the gifts she'd bought from the mail-order catalog. On Christmas Eve, the family gathered in the parlor for some hot chocolate and to listen to Laura read *A Christmas Carol* by Charles Dickens. Once the children had been settled down and tucked in for the night, Laura, Ian, and Fiona set out the gifts under the tree.

"You needn't have bought gifts for everyone, Laura," Fiona said. "That certainly was not expected of you."

"Oh, but I wanted to, ma'am. I just love giving gifts, and with the mail-order catalog, it was no problem at all. Besides, they are not elaborate gifts by any means."

"I'm sure the children will appreciate whatever you bought for them," Fiona said as she turned and left to go back to her cottage.

Laura decided to take this opportunity to speak to Ian to see if she could determine what made him so angry and always upset with Reuben.

"Could I have a word with you, sir?" Laura approached Ian who was fussing with something under the tree.

"It's getting late, Laura. Can't it wait until another time?"

"I suppose it could, but I would rather just have my say and be done with it."

"Very well. What is it?"

"I'm concerned about Reuben and how you always seem to think the worst about him. I realize it may not be my place, sir, but insofar as it affects Reuben and his learning, I feel I must say something."

"You are right that it is not your place, but you do need to understand that Reuben is a crafty, willful young man who apparently has you wrapped around his finger much as he does my mother."

"Could it be possible that you have blinders on when it comes to your son? I have seen nothing to indicate that he is willful or devious. He is just a very bright boy who desperately wants to win your approval, which you seem unwilling to provide."

In the silence that ensued, Laura felt she might have just overstepped her boundaries and hoped she had not angered Ian on the eve of an important holiday. She was about to turn and leave the room when Ian hung his head and said, "Reuben and his mother were very close, and ever since her death, he seems to blame me. I'm not sure what gave him that impression, but before you arrived, he was always argumentative and running away when things didn't go his way. I guess I have just gotten used to his antics and expect they will continue."

"But don't you see, sir? If you expect him to misbehave, then that is what he will do. Some positive encouragement from you would go a long way to improving his behavior."

Ian's tone indicated he was not really sure it was possible. "I will consider what you have told me, Laura. But for now, I feel I must turn in for the night. The children will be up early and eager to get into their gifts. Good night."

"Good night, sir." Laura watched him head upstairs before turning out the lights and going up to bed herself. She hoped she had made her point clear to Ian and hadn't jeopardized her job in the process.

Chapter 15

CHRISTMAS MORNING BROUGHT THE usual chaos of excited children unwrapping gifts while the adults tried to keep the pandemonium to a minimum. The children, each in turn, gave Laura a grateful hug after opening the gift she had given them. Bridget was so delighted to discover her doll was dressed in a fashionable outfit with a pretty porcelain face. Cassie's eyes filled with tears as she inspected the easel, which Laura had assembled, and Reuben could hardly wait to read all about the adventures of Huckleberry Finn.

In turn, each of the children was captivated as they watched Laura unwrap the handmade gifts they had each made for her. Bridget had cut out a snowflake and wrapped it. Cassie had, of course, created a lovely drawing of the ocean for her. Reuben had put together a frame for Cassie's drawing and painted it blue to go with the décor in her room.

"Thank you so much for these lovely gifts." Laura herself was on the verge of tears. "And thank you, Ian and Fiona, for the riding skirt and boots. Looks like I really must learn to ride now."

"Besides the wagons, riding horseback is the main mode of transportation, so knowing how to ride is essential, I'm afraid," said Ian. "And I'd like to thank you for the lovely ink pen. It will come in handy when I do my books."

Fiona was apparently pleased with her lacy black Spanish shawl as she put it on and wore it all day. Manuel and Consuela did not join the family for opening gifts but were very appreciative to Laura later in the day for the things she had given them. All in all, Laura decided her first Christmas in her new home had been a success, even if there weren't any snow or sleigh rides. She was looking forward to what new things she would learn in the coming year.

*****

As the new year began, the family's routine got back to normal. Laura spent her days tutoring the children and helping them in any way she could to navigate the lessons she prepared. Bridget was having less trouble with her numbers, while Cassie spent any chance she could get experimenting with the various color paints her grandmother had given her using the easel Laura gave her for Christmas.

Reuben's time at the rancho was complete, which meant he was spending much more time in the classroom with the girls. Laura found him to be eager to learn new things and was constantly having to come up with ideas to keep him challenged.

One day, while the girls were busy with their mathematics problems, Laura asked Reuben to join her out on the veranda.

"What's this about?" he inquired. "Did I do something wrong?"

"No, of course not. You needn't think that you are always in trouble."

"Well, usually I am, so I can't help wondering what I did now."

"First of all, Reuben, you are not in trouble. I just wanted to see if I can get you to help me with something."

"Anything for you, Miss Laura. What do you need?"

"I've been trying to figure out why your father always thinks the worst of you and wondered if you had any thoughts on the matter."

"Well, you do know he is not my real father, don't you?"

"Yes, your grandmother told me that your real father died when you were just a baby and that Ian married your mother and adopted you."

"My real father turned out to be an outlaw, and I think father is afraid I will be just like him."

"But there is no reason to assume anything like that at all. You have been raised by a loving mother and, I might add, by him."

"Since Mom died, he just doesn't seem to trust me. Sometimes, I think he believes I somehow was involved with the gang that killed her. Honestly, Miss Laura, I don't have anything to do with outlaws and I don't even know who they are."

Laura dismissed Reuben to go back in with his sisters while she contemplated how to approach Ian about his misplaced distrust and how it was affecting a sweet, young boy.

*****

Before long, the rains of January had abated, and signs of spring were beginning to appear. Although there were no clearly defined seasons as Laura had experienced in the east, there were subtle changes evident in this moderate climate. Because of the restoration work that had been done to the mission by the Landmarks Club, the mission became a destination for travelers. Tourists came not only to wander through every nook and cranny of the mission but to paint and photograph it as well.

As part of their history and art lessons, Laura gained permission to take the children to the mission for an outing one pleasant spring day. Consuela packed them a picnic lunch, and Manuel hitched the horse to one of the buggies. Cassie brought along her paints, while Bridget settled for crayons and some paper. Reuben tried his best to appear bored by the entire trip, but Laura could tell he was just as anxious to wander through the old mission as she was.

The mission was now just a picturesque ruin. Earthquake, neglect, and vandalism had reduced what once was the noblest of mission churches to a mockery of its former grandeur. Without caretaker or inhabitant, its empty courts and corridors fell prey to the whim of vagrant and vandal. Irreverent goats collected near a broken adobe wall were briskly nosing out tidbits of straw and chaff.

"Won't this be a marvelous setting for one of your paintings, Cassie?" Laura gazed in awe at the wild flowers that had sunk their roots in the cracks of the desolated sanctuary's wall and were brightly blooming. High up under the broken eaves of the nave, swallows had built their mud nests.

"But it's just a fallen-down old building," protested Reuben. "Why would anyone want to do a painting of that?"

"Think of all the history, Reuben, that hides behind the surface rubble."

"History is boring!"

"Have you studied a lot of history, Reuben? It is often very interesting to learn what happened and how it led to what we know and do today."

"Like what?'

"For example, this mission was established in 1776 by Father Junipero Serra, a Franciscan padre who was in charge of setting up a chain of missions in California to gather the Indians into settlements and teach them to be self-sufficient."

"What makes that so interesting?"

"Spanish culture was becoming dominant in California, and the Franciscans feared the local Indians and their culture would be in jeopardy. They hoped the missions would serve as tools to aid the Indians in making the transition to the new culture."

"Did that help?"

"Not really, and many conflicts arose before the mission was finally completed. Additionally, the land attached to the mission was to be held in trust for the Indians who, when they were ready, would take over its ownership."

"So the Indians really own the mission?"

"No. Though many of the Indians lived in the mission compound or near it, they were never able to make the transition to land ownership."

"Did they destroy the mission?" asked Bridget.

"No, dummy. It was an earthquake!" Reuben replied.

"I am not a dummy, Reuben," said Bridget.

"No one is a dummy. Reuben, don't be so sharp with your sister." Laura continued, "Once the church was built, with the help of the Indians, it stood for only six years until a massive earthquake in 1812 toppled the building to the ground."

"Was anyone in the church when it collapsed?" asked Cassie.

"Actually, yes. A mass was being held, and while some were able to escape, some forty people were buried under the rubble. The building has never been fully restored."

"I thought a group called the Landmarks Club were planning to preserve the mission?" suggested Cassie.

"They have done some renovations, but there is still much to be done." Laura began to gather her things and stood up. "I think that is enough of a history lesson for today. Why don't we find a nice sunny spot and have ourselves a picnic lunch?"

After lunch, Cassie picked out a nice spot and began sketching the ruins and surrounding vegetation. Laura sat nearby, reading to Bridget who had laid her head on Laura's lap and then promptly fell asleep. Reuben wandered aimlessly through the inner patio ruins, wondering about the many rumors he had heard about tunnels or underground passages that ran beneath the mission that had been used by the Franciscan fathers to hide valuables and wealth. He wondered if any of the treasure was still there.

It seemed all too soon to Laura that it was time to pack everything into the buggy and head back to Walnut Hill. The soft glow of the declining sun was bringing out the magic of soft color on the arches and accentuating the ancient carvings with edges of purple shadow. All in all, she felt it had been a good day of study for them all, and she was quite impressed with Reuben's inquisitiveness, even if it did come in the form of rebellion.

Chapter 16

FOLLOWING THE EASTER SUNDAY mass, Fiona announced that she planned to take the train to San Diego to visit relatives and was taking Bridget and Cassie with her. While Consuela and Fiona got the girls' things packed, Laura set about putting together some lessons the girls could work on while they were away.

"How come we have to do schoolwork while we are on vacation?" Bridget whined.

"It's not difficult work, just something to keep you busy when you don't have anything better to do. Besides, you will be further ahead in your studies and won't have to make it up when you get back."

"Good. Because we plan to be back in time for La Fiesta de Ocho Dias in June," Cassie added.

"What is La Fiesta de Ocho Dias?"

"The eight-day festival. It is like a farmers' fair. The farmers display products from their gardens in booths. Then the priest, followed by six small girls dressed in white, visits each booth and awards prizes. After this ceremony, there is a bullfight in the town plaza, followed by a feast in which all the food is donated by the folks of San Juan Capistrano. In the evening, there is a fandango featuring many lively Spanish dances," explained Cassie.

"Wow, that sounds like a lot of fun, except for the bullfight. I don't think I would like that too much."

"Mama didn't like the bullfights much either," said Bridget. "But she really liked the dancing. She was a really good dancer."

All that was a couple of months away, and Laura needed to turn her thoughts to what she should be doing while the girls were gone. Her thoughts were also on Reuben and whether he felt left out in some way, but she soon learned that he was going to be working on the Valencia rancho, not as punishment but because he wanted to.

Apparently, his sojourn at the ranch during his period of punishment gave him a taste for ranching. Perhaps, Laura thought, it was more likely that Reuben enjoyed being with Dylan and that was the reason for his interest in ranching.

While at the train station, after seeing Fiona and the girls off, Laura noticed the train schedule and the times the train traveled to Santa Ana, the county seat. Suddenly, she thought it had been a long time since she had gone to a doctor and was wondering if she should go for a checkup. She was feeling much better, but it couldn't hurt to know for sure.

Since the only doctor was in Santa Ana, she would make an appointment for a checkup, and while there, she might do a little shopping. However, more than shopping, she wanted to go to the newspaper office to see if she could find anything about the attack on Maria or the search for the outlaws. On the day of her appointment, Manuel drove Laura to the train station.

"Are you sure you don't want me to come along, Miss Laura?"

"No, Manuel. You have work to do back at the grove. I'll be just fine."

"But I'm not sure it is a good idea for a young woman to travel alone."

"She won't be alone," Dylan said as he walked up to where they were standing on the platform.

"What are you doing here?" Laura's irritation was quite evident. "I don't need a chaperone. I traveled all the way from Boston by myself. I'm certainly able to handle a trip to Santa Ana."

"No one doubts you can handle the trip, but since I had to go to Santa Ana myself, I just thought we could enjoy each other's company along the way."

"Well, I can't tell you not to go to Santa Ana, but I have no intention of enjoying your company. What do you have to do that is so important?"

"I'm not sure that is pertinent, but I have some business to attend to for Senor Valencia." Dylan turned and stepped onto the train. "I think we had better get settled. The train is ready to leave."

Laura was not happy about spending the entire trip with Dylan, but the idea of making a public scene was far more repugnant to her. Once they were settled in their seats and the train began leaving the station, Laura stared out the window in an attempt to let Dylan know she was not in the mood to talk. They traveled in silence for several miles before Dylan attempted to engage her in conversation.

"Manuel told me you were going to the doctor in Santa Ana. Are you ill?"

"No, but I need to have a checkup periodically because of my asthma. I came here because my doctor back east felt this climate might be better for me. I just need to find out how I'm doing."

"Well, your trips to the hot springs should be helping you too."

"That's what I hope to find out. Now, if you don't mind, I'd like to read for a while."

Dylan nodded his agreement and left her to her reading. Before too long, he noticed she was staring out the window much more than she was reading. A smile crossed his face as he said, "That book must not be very interesting."

"Why would you say that?"

"You have spent more time looking out the window than you have reading."

"I find the countryside here fascinating. Rolling hills with strange vegetation and barely any trees. It is so different from the east where I'm from."

"I can imagine that life in general is far different from where you were raised. Do you find it difficult to adjust?"

"Life certainly is different. I have enjoyed learning a lot of new things, but often, I miss some of the things I had back home."

"Like what?"

"The most significant change for me is the lack of defined seasons, particularly the winter season. I miss the sight of snow on the fir trees and the holiday decorations that go up every year."

"But on the other hand, you don't have to shovel snow and worry about heating and such."

"I suppose you are right, but here, you have the unrelenting sun and the Santa Ana winds to contend with."

"I guess no place is absolutely ideal. I came out from Chicago, and I have to say I do not miss those winters at all."

"I didn't realize you were not from this area. How long have you been here?"

"I've been at the rancho for nearly a year now. Before that, I worked in San Diego for a couple of years."

"Wasn't Mrs. Castle from San Diego? I think the girls told me that."

"I don't know. I guess she could have been." Dylan looked past Laura out the window. "Looks like we'll be in Santa Ana soon."

Laura returned to her book, but she couldn't help thinking Dylan had changed the subject rather abruptly and she wondered why. Had he known Maria Castle before? No, that didn't make sense if he had only been here less than a year. Still, there was something he was hiding. She was sure of it.

The visit with the doctor went well, and Laura was told that her health was improving. The doctor indicated that spending time at the hot springs was an excellent idea and suggested she do it as much as possible. She asked him whether horseback riding could adversely affect her asthma, hoping he would tell her not to do it. On the contrary, he said that horseback riding itself could do no harm. He just admonished her to stay away from the wheat and straw in the stables as the dust could cause a coughing fit.

As Laura left the doctor's office, she asked the nurse where she could find the newspaper office.

"The *Santa Ana Register* is over on Fourth Street. That's just one block up that way," she said, pointing to her right. "And then a block to the left. You can't miss it. There's usually a bunch of old men standing out front trying to look important."

Laura thanked her and headed in the direction of Fourth Street. When she reached the newspaper office, she became very aware of what the nurse had said about men standing around. Using all the resolve she could muster, Laura walked up to the front door and went in. Several of the men doffed their hats as she walked by them, and she nodded politely in return. Once inside, she found a young woman standing behind a long counter.

"May I help you?" the woman asked as Laura walked up to the counter.

"I hope so," Laura said hesitantly. She hadn't really thought out how to proceed once she got there. "I work for the Castle family in San Juan Capistrano, and I was wondering if you had any information on the death of Mrs. Castle or the investigation."

"What did you say the name was again?"

"Castle. Maria Castle from San Juan Capistrano."

"And about when would this have happened? Do you know?"

Laura realized she did not know exactly when it had happened but said, "I think it was about two years ago, but I don't know the exact date."

"Let me see what I can find. Wait here a moment."

The woman went over to a file of some sort, while Laura worried she could get in trouble for asking about the Castles. She would just have to say she was on some sort of errand for Mr. Castle and hope she could get away with checking things out. Within a few minutes, the lady was back with a copy of several newspapers, which she set on the counter in front of Laura.

"These are the papers from two years ago. Anything that was reported should be in there."

"Thank you very much," Laura said as she began to leaf through the papers.

After going through several papers, she came across the notice of Maria's death. She noted the date and realized Bridget had only been three when her mother died. All the article said was it was believed that outlaws had invaded the property while Mrs. Castle was home alone and had apparently been killed by them.

One theory was that the outlaws believed Mrs. Castle was in possession of something her former husband had taken from them, and they wanted it back. When she could not produce what they were searching for, they killed her. Laura continued looking through the papers to see if anything had been reported about a follow-up investigation but found nothing that indicated anyone was looking into it.

"Thank you for allowing me to look through these papers," Laura said as she pushed them across the counter.

"Do you need copies of anything? We have copy clerks that can copy the information for you."

"That won't be necessary. I found what I was looking for. Thank you very much for your help."

As Laura left the *Santa Ana Register*, she realized she would not have time for any shopping and so she headed to the train station to wait for the next train, which was due within the half hour. As she approached the station, Dylan fell in beside her and began walking with her.

"You look rather solemn," said Dylan. "Bad news at the doctor's office?"

"What? Oh no. He gave me a clean bill of health." Laura continued to walk with her head down as though deep in thought.

Dylan walked silently beside her for a few paces, then said, "So why the long face?"

Laura appeared at first not to have heard him but then absentmindedly answered, "Just trying to figure something out that doesn't quite make sense."

"I saw you coming out of the newspaper office. Did something happen there that has you so perplexed? And what were doing there in the first place?"

"I went there to check the newspaper's records, and yes, I am very puzzled about something." Laura sat on a bench outside the train station, and Dylan joined her.

"Why on earth would you need to check the newspapers?"

"I was trying to see if I could find out anything about Maria Castle's death. Reuben seems so upset by it, and I thought if I could get some information, perhaps I could help him better deal with it."

"Did you get your question answered?"

Just then, the train pulled into the station, and Laura and Dylan boarded it for the trip back to Capistrano. Laura did not even object when Dylan opted to usher her to a seat and sit beside her. She was still trying to figure out why there didn't seem to have been any investigation into Maria's death.

Once the train pulled away from the station, Dylan again asked, "So did you get an answer to your question?"

"I think I ended up with more questions and very few answers. The newspaper account for Maria simply states she was killed by outlaws who were looking for something."

"And you find that confusing for some reason?" Now Dylan seemed confused.

"That is not what I found confusing. That is pretty much what Ian, I mean Mr. Castle, told me."

Laura was not sure why she was discussing this with Dylan, but she really needed to talk to someone. And since he was not a family member, perhaps he could give her an objective point of view.

"Dare I ask why you are confused, or are you going to bite my head off like before?"

Ignoring his snide comment, Laura said, "There doesn't seem to be any record of an investigation or that anyone is trying to find the killers. I don't understand."

Not sure if he should reply, Dylan forged ahead anyway. "That is very simple. The investigation has been turned over to the Pinkerton agency, which is a private investigation firm."

They sat in silence for several minutes, when Laura suddenly looked at Dylan and asked again how he knew all this information. It didn't seem like something folks would talk casually about to a relative stranger.

"You seem to know a lot of intimate details of the Castles' lives. Just who are you?"

Dylan sat thoughtfully for a few seconds, then decided to tell Laura the details she was looking for. "I want to tell you something, but I would like you to keep it in the strictest confidence."

"What? This sounds very serious."

"It is serious. I am actually a Pinkerton agent from Chicago, and I was hired by Ian to work undercover as a vaquero on the Valencia rancho in order to gather information regarding the group of men who are thought to be the gang who killed Maria."

Laura was stunned but said, "Surely you don't suspect the Mexicans that work on the ranchero. Most of them have worked there for years and passed along the privilege to younger generations."

"Yes, but there have been some newer ones who come along from time to time. Ian doesn't believe the rancho vaqueros are directly involved with the outlaws, but they could possibly know something of the men who might be involved."

The train was pulling into the Capistrano station, and as they gathered their things in preparation to disembark, Dylan turned to Laura and said, "I trust you will keep this information to yourself. I still have a lot to discover before this case is closed, and I don't want to let folks know exactly who I am for a while. And if you should hear or see anything suspicious, I'd appreciate it if you would let me know."

"You mean you want me to spy?"

"No, but who knows what you might hear or see that could be of value. I assume you would want to help stop these outlaws if you could."

Laura wasn't sure how helpful she could be, but she agreed to keep his secret and to pass on any information that might be of use, if she came across any. Manuel was waiting at the station to take her home, and as they rode out of town, she couldn't help wondering what else could crop up to surprise her.

Chapter 17

WITH REUBEN WORKING AT the rancho and Ian busy with the walnut business, Laura spent most of her time working on new lesson plans for when the children returned. Consuela had been so glad to hear that Laura's health was improving and asked if Laura would like to learn how to cook some of the Mexican dishes that she seemed to enjoy so much.

Therefore, many afternoons were spent in the kitchen rolling out tortillas, making quesadillas, and learning to make guacamole. Laura's favorite snack was warm quesadillas dipped in guacamole. It became her afternoon ritual to sit on the veranda with a glass of agua frescas (literally fresh waters), a refreshing fruit drink, and her quesadillas.

One afternoon, as she lingered on the veranda, Dylan rode up with Sophie in hand. Laura tensed as she feared this was going to be another riding lesson.

"How would you like to ride out to see some of the surrounding area?"

"While a tour sounds marvelous, I'm still not very comfortable on a horse."

"No time like the present to practice getting comfortable. And it would be good for you to know the area around here."

After some hesitation, Laura consented and took her dishes into the house. While she changed into her riding clothes, she wondered if Dylan had an ulterior motive for riding through the surrounding hillsides.

Laura found it much easier to get on the horse this time, especially since she had put on her new riding skirt and boots. She was very tentative at first, but with Dylan's guidance, she carefully rode down the hill to the road that led toward San Juan Point. Before long, Laura was feeling fairly confident, though she realized a lot of that confidence came from trusting the horse not to do something wild and crazy.

"You're doing very well. Are you more comfortable?"

"I think Sophie makes me feel comfortable because she seems to know what I need."

"Indeed. Horses are very intuitive about their riders. If you are fearful, they can sense that. If you are feeling confident, they know that too."

"I never thought about animals sensing things as we do. That's very interesting."

"Do you feel comfortable enough to canter for a ways?" With that, Dylan nudged his horse to a canter, and Sophie copied his gait.

"Wait, I didn't say I was that confident!" Laura shouted to be heard as Dylan rode several yards ahead of her.

"You better hurry up and get confident because Sophie is trying to keep up with Bandit here."

"Your horse's name is Bandit? Are you serious?"

"Yep! Pretty appropriate, don't you think?"

Laura merely shook her head as she cantered along next to the Pinkerton man and his horse, Bandit. As they approached San Juan Point, Dylan turned south along the ocean, and Laura followed.

"Where are we going?" she asked.

"I want to show you where the little town called San Juan-by-the-Sea used to be."

"Is it a ghost town? I've heard about ghost towns in the west."

"It used to be a place where society held picnics and attended dances and Sunday bullfights. But sadly, now, only the water tank, an unsightly barn, and what was known at the old Dutch Hall remain."

"What happened to it?"

"In 1887, there was a brief land boom, which ended as quickly as it started. Land prices became inflated, banks stopped loaning money on unimproved real estate, and buyers began to disappear. Soon, what had been a prosperous area fell to ruins."

"So what is there to see, then?"

"I'm just interested in checking out the area. It could be possible to purchase some land there now at a reasonable price."

"Why would you want to purchase land in an area that is in ruins? That doesn't make sense."

"I personally believe the area will be rebuilt in the future, and by purchasing land now, it could be worth a lot more in the future."

"Seems pretty risky to me. Maybe it's my New England upbringing that keeps me from wanting to do anything risky."

"You're not in New England anymore, and the west has been built on folks taking risks. I try to be sure my risks are based on some sound information, however."

"That seems prudent."

After they had ridden around what used to be a thriving little coastal town, they headed back toward Walnut Hill. She and Dylan talked about mundane topics on the ride home. Dylan asked Laura about her cooking lessons and what else she had been doing to fill her time while school was not in session. She told him about her disasters in the kitchen while learning to make tortillas, which made them both have a good laugh.

By the time they reached the big house on the hill, they were having a civil conversation. Dylan helped Laura off her horse and thanked her for a lovely afternoon as he took Sophie's reins and trotted off toward Valencia Rancho. Laura watched him go wondering why one minute, she loathed the man, and the next found she enjoyed his easy company. With that thought, she turned and climbed the steps to the veranda where she found Ian sitting with a drink, smoking a cigar.

"I see you've been out riding with our friendly vaquero." Ian's tone was verging on accusatory.

"Yes. He thought I could use another riding lesson, and since the doctor told me I should spend as much time in the fresh air as I could, I decided to combine the two activities."

Laura began to turn to go into the house when Ian suddenly said, "Are you falling for the charms of our local bad boy?"

"I beg your pardon?" exclaimed Laura.

"You two seem to be getting pretty cozy of late. Manuel tells me you rode to and from Santa Ana on the train a couple of weeks ago."

Laura was not sure what had brought on this particular tone of questioning. It seemed almost as if Ian were jealous.

"Sir, I'm not sure what you are implying, but there is only one train a day to Santa Ana and one return trip, so if we both had business in Santa Ana, it stands to reason we would be on the same train."

"That may be, but I think you would be wise to keep your distance from that young man. We don't know much about him, except that he seems to roam all over the country doing odd jobs when it suits him. I just don't want to see you get hurt when he packs up and takes off again."

"Rest assured, sir. I couldn't care less if Dylan Laughlin leaves town tomorrow." Turning on her heel, Laura stomped into the house and went directly upstairs to her room. It was obvious Ian didn't realize she knew who Dylan really was.

Chapter 18

THE NEXT MORNING, FOLLOWING a breakfast of huevos rancheros, Laura decided to spend some time in the solarium. Just as she was headed out of the dining area, Consuela called to her.

"Would you like to learn how to make some albondigas soup? I'm making a batch to have on hand for quick meals."

"Is that the soup I had the night I arrived?"

"Si, the Mexican meatball soup. Is very delicious and easy to make."

"Sounds yummy, but I have some work to do in the solarium that I have been putting off for far too long. Perhaps we can do it the next time you make the soup?"

"Very well, then, senorita. But it may be a long time before I make the soup again."

Laura nodded and proceeded down the hallway to the stairs. When she reached the landing for the second floor, she thought about how hard it had been for her to stand up to Ian and yet how well it had turned out. She had been certain he was going to fire her. Instead of continuing on to the solarium, she decided to see whether Consuela had started preparing the soup. Perhaps she could learn a new recipe and find out more while they cooked together.

"Have you started your albon...your soup yet?" Laura asked as she entered the kitchen. "It seems I didn't have as much to do as I thought I had."

"I was just gathering some of the ingredients. Come, put on an apron, and we will make albondigas soup together."

Consuela was very patient giving instructions as they went along while Laura wrote them down in her black-and-white composition book. She was collecting a book full of new recipes for use some time in the future. She had no idea what she would be doing after the children were grown or, for that matter, if Ian decided to let her go from her position here.

"Can I ask you a question, Consuela?"

"Of course, you can ask me anything. I can see something is troubling you. What is the matter?"

"Why did Ian keep the solarium closed up, not allowing anyone but you to enter?"

"Senor Ian kept it as a shrine to his wife. I think sometime in the evening, he took a bottle of spirits and went in there to cry."

"How awful for him. I would think it is better now that it is open so that he and the children can remember happier times with Maria."

"He did not see it like that, I guess, until you talked him into using it for the children. He was devastated when Senora Maria passed away. I'm not sure he will ever get over her death."

"Keeping her memory locked up like that was surely not the way to do it. Do you know how she died? No one seems eager to talk of her death."

"It is not known exactly what happened. She was here alone one day, and when Senor Ian came home, he found her. Some say that the outlaws who killed her first husband rode through here and killed Senora Maria before searching the house and riding on."

"Was anything taken?"

"No, I don't think so. They were apparently looking for something. Drawers had been searched, and things were thrown about, but no one knows for sure."

Laura decided to change the subject so as not to appear too inquisitive. "When are Fiona and the girls planning to return? Do you know?"

"Si. Senora Fiona sent a telegram to say they will be coming back next week. She said the girls are excited about getting back for the festival."

"It will be nice to have them back. I must confess I have missed them more than I thought I would. I have become very fond of Bridget and Cassie and Reuben as well."

"Reuben has changed a lot since you have come. I think you are a good influence on him."

"Well, thank you for those kind words, Consuela. But Reuben has been responsible for any changes you see in him. I have merely facilitated his progress. He just needed some encouragement."

"Si, senorita. Si."

They continued their cooking lesson and tasted the result of their efforts. Laura was amazed at how delicious the soup was. "I don't know what I was expecting, but this is delicious.'

Consuela simply smiled and began to clean the pots and utensils they had used in cooking. After Laura finished helping Consuela clean up, she took her book that was filling up with exotic recipes and went upstairs to her room. She felt a little shudder as she passed the closed door to the solarium and wondered if perhaps Maria preferred the children using her room now as opposed to the manner in which Ian had been utilizing it.

Once in her room, Laura finished planning the children's lessons for when the girls returned from their trip and Reuben finished his work at the rancho. But she couldn't seem to concentrate. Frustrated, she left her desk and lay down on the bed where she promptly fell asleep. She was awakened suddenly and realized she had been dreaming. It had seemed so real, she wasn't sure at first where she was. Then, she realized there was someone lightly knocking on her door, and that was what had awakened her.

She stood, straightened her dress, and opened the door to find Ian standing there. *Oh no*, she thought. *He's going to let me go before Fiona returns with the girls.* However, she calmly asked, "Is there something you need?"

"Yes, Miss Palmer. I believe I owe you an apology for my behavior the other day. It's just that I have known men like Dylan Laughlin, and they are not to be trusted."

"I am sorry you do not trust me to handle myself in such situations, but you have nothing to worry about. I'm just curious to learn more about him."

"Well, you know what they say about what curiosity did to the cat. Nevertheless, I was rude, and I just wanted to apologize to you in person. I also wanted to let you know that I will be gone for a few days on business but should be back in time to greet Fiona and the girls. I will need you to keep a close eye on Reuben for me while I'm gone."

"That won't be a problem, sir. Reuben and I get along just fine."

Ian turned and headed toward his room on the floor below, leaving Laura standing there wondering what just happened. What kind of trip was he going on? Did it really matter? She found she actually felt a sense of relief. She shook her head, closed the door, and returned to her lesson planning.

Later, when she went down to help Consuela with the evening meal, she learned that Ian had already ridden off to wherever he was going. Laura and Reuben enjoyed a hearty bowl of albondigas and warm tortillas at the table on the veranda. The days were staying a bit warmer longer into the evenings, making an outdoor meal quite pleasant.

They chatted about Reuben's day at the rancho. Laura noticed he was very excited to be able to ramble on about what he had done all day without someone treating his stories as inconsequential. When he asked about her day, she told him about learning how to make the soup and about lesson planning but did not mention anything about his father's apology.

Chapter 19

FIONA AND THE GIRLS returned the following week as predicted. The girls were bubbling over with tales of their trip, their visit with their aunts, and all the wonderful things they had experienced. Laura worried that Reuben would feel left out, but he was caught up in their excitement and shared some of his experiences at the rancho. It appeared the entire family atmosphere was more pleasant and contained less tension when Ian was away.

Bridget couldn't wait to show Laura the new books she got and how well she could read them. "I'm a really good reader now, Miss Laura."

"Yes, you are. Now how much math did you learn while you were away?" Laura teased.

"We were on a holiday, Miss Laura, not away at school." Bridget pouted.

"I was only joking, dear. I did not expect you to be studying while you were away, but you may have to write me a story about your adventure when we get back to classes."

Not to be left out, Cassie showed Laura the drawings she did while on her trip.

"My goodness, Cassie, I think these are magnificent. You are getting better all the time. I really like what you've done with the colors and the shading. Good work!"

"Thank you, Miss Laura. One of the aunts has a friend who paints, and she showed me some tricks to make the drawings better."

"These are good enough to be shown and perhaps sold at La Fiesta de Ochos Dias," Laura said, holding one up for everyone to see.

"Do you really think so?" Cassie looked at her grandmother, then at Laura.

"She may be absolutely right, Cassie," said her grandmother. "I just never thought of doing something like that. Perhaps we can put them on display at our walnut booth and see what happens."

"That's a splendid idea." Laura put her arm across Cassie's shoulders and gave her a little hug.

"What if Daddy says no?" Cassie suddenly asked.

"You let me worry about your father, Cassie," said Fiona. "I can handle him, if need be."

Laura was quite certain that Fiona indeed could handle Ian. She gave Cassie another squeeze and sent the girls off to play outside for a while.

Fiona turned to Laura and asked how things went while they were gone. Laura shrugged and told her about her trip to the doctor in Santa Ana and about riding out to San Juan-by-the-Sea with Dylan, but she did not mention Ian's attitude about Dylan when she returned.

"Is Ian around somewhere? I'd like to let him know we are back and give him some news I learned while I was away."

"Mr. Castle left last week on a business trip of some kind."

"Ian and his little business trips," exclaimed Fiona. "Did he not know we were coming back this week?"

"Yes, I'm sure he did, but it seemed to be something of an urgent matter."

"Ian's trips are rarely urgent, but they do seem to be of great importance to him. You know, he was away when his wife died. I can't help wondering whether things would have turned out differently if he had been here." Fiona shook her head in a frustrated manner and turned to go to her cottage.

Laura couldn't help wondering what hold Fiona must have over Ian and what on earth she meant by "his little trips." There was definitely something going on, an undercurrent of some kind. Perhaps she should mention all this to Dylan the next time she saw him. Maybe he had some idea of where Ian went periodically and what this all meant.

*****

Ian returned from his trip a few days later with no mention of where he had been. Of course, it would have been difficult to get a word in edgewise with the girls regaling him with stories of their trip. He even listened to Reuben talk of his work at the ranch, which made Laura wonder if he was deliberately avoiding any conversation regarding his travel. Since it was not her place to inquire and since she was on shaky footing anyway with Ian, she made no mention of his trip either.

Life seemed to get back to normal with the exception of planning for the upcoming festival. With Fiona's help, Cassie was able to convince her father to allow her to place some of her drawings in their booth. Ian was reluctant at first but finally consented.

"I just don't want you to be disappointed if no one is interested in buying your drawings," he said.

"You seem to be assuming that they are not worthy of being sold," Fiona scolded. "Perhaps you should not be surprised if they do sell."

Since her riding skills were improving immensely, Laura had asked Reuben to see whether Sophie could be brought to Walnut Hill so that she could have the horse available if she should take a notion to go for a ride. Dylan was happy to oblige, and Reuben was delighted that he would be put in charge of taking care of the horse for her.

So on an afternoon when everyone was otherwise occupied, Laura decided to ride out to the hillside above the ocean. It was one of her favorite spots, and though she didn't really expect to see Dylan, she rather hoped that he might be out riding and they would have a chance to chat. She wanted to tell him about Ian's mysterious trips and ask him if he knew anything about them. But as she stood atop the hill overlooking the ocean, she realized that Dylan was nowhere around that day and their chat would have to wait until some other time.

As she was about to head back to Walnut Hill, she noticed some strange activity down near the base of the hill near the water. She watched for a few minutes trying to decide what was going on when she noticed a couple of men disappear into what appeared to be an opening in the side of the hill. *There must be a cave or tunnel down there*, she thought. Maybe it had something to do with the outlaws she'd heard about from Dylan. When the men did not reappear, Laura turned her horse around and headed to the house. On her way, she noticed Dylan riding toward the rancho. She waved, but he apparently didn't see her as he kept going at top speed.

"Wonder what he's in such a hurry about," she said out loud to herself and continued back to the stable.

Reuben was waiting for her when she returned; and he took the horse, unsaddled it, and led it to the barn. Laura watched as he carefully placed some oats in a pail for the horse and added water to the trough so that Sophie could get a drink.

When Reuben noticed Laura watching him, he said, "Dylan told me I had to take good care of Sophie or else he would take her back to the rancho."

"I'd say you are doing an excellent job, and I do appreciate it. I would hate to lose Sophie now that I'm getting used to riding her."

Laura left Reuben to his chores and went into the house. Consuela was busy preparing the evening meal and said she didn't need any help when Laura asked. Just as Laura was about to head upstairs to get ready for supper, Ian stepped out of his office and asked her to join him for a bit. She reluctantly went into his office, not knowing quite what to expect. Was he going to let her go after all? Her hands became sweaty, and she wiped them on her skirt as she sat in the chair he motioned her to.

"I take it you have been out riding."

"Yes. It was such a lovely day, and everyone was occupied with some project or another. So I decided to get some air and ride over to look at the ocean. Is there a problem?"

"No, no! Your riding seems to be coming along nicely. Is Dylan still giving you riding lessons?"

"Not really. Since I have been doing well on my own, he has let me take Sophie out alone. And thank you for allowing him to keep Sophie here so that I can do that."

Ian nodded and looked down at something on his desk. There was obviously something on his mind, and Laura wished that he would just get to it. She was getting more anxious by the minute.

Finally, he looked up and said, "I'm pleased to hear you are not spending so much time with Dylan Laughlin these days."

"Sir, I—"

"As I've indicated before, I don't think it wise for you to become so attached to our handsome vaquero. Who knows what he might be up to or why, but I do not trust the man and I would hate for you to set your cap for him, only to be hurt in the end."

"Sir, you can be assured I have no plans to 'set my cap' for Dylan or anyone else for that matter." Laura still wondered if Ian was truly concerned or if his attitude was one of a jealous nature.

Ian quietly indicated that was all, and Laura left. She was acutely aware that her talk with him had brought questions to mind about his motives, so she decided to keep an eye out for what might be behind his concern.

Before long, it was time for La Fiesta de Ocho Dias, and preparations were made to travel to Capistrano and set up the booth that would feature the walnuts from the Walnut Hill orchards. Reuben had even made more frames so that Cassie's drawings would seem more professional. The entire household seemed to buzz with excitement.

Laura did not know exactly what to expect, but on the first day of the festival, she found that Cassie's description of a farmer's fair was very accurate. Wandering among the various booths, Laura was amazed at all the produce that came from the local farms, and she thoroughly enjoyed the ceremony performed by the priest followed by the six small girls dressed in white who sang lovely songs and scattered petals along the way. Prizes were awarded to the best booth, and Laura was especially happy to see that the Walnut Hill booth was awarded one of the prizes.

She walked over to the booth to see how Cassie's drawings were being received, only to notice there were none there. It made Laura angry to think that, after telling Cassie she could put her work in the booth, Ian had obviously changed his mind. When she found Cassie, she didn't look at all disappointed as Laura imagined she would be.

"Why didn't you get to put your drawings in the booth?" Laura asked Cassie.

"Oh, but I did, Miss Laura. I've already sold all of them. Isn't that great?"

"It certainly is, Cassie. You must be so proud." Laura felt a huge relief that Cassie had not been disappointed by her father and gave her a big hug.

"I'm on my way to find Grandmother and Bridget. Want to come along?"

"Of course. Where are they? Do you think…"

"I imagine they are somewhere near the food. It's about time for the feast to begin. C'mon!"

Cassie grabbed Laura's hand, and they worked their way through the crowd to the tables being set with all the food that had been donated for the occasion. Laura spotted Consuela with some of the other Mexican ladies, dishing up casseroles, salads, and meats. It truly was going to be a feast for sure. About that time, Fiona and Bridget appeared, and they all found seats at the table together with Ian and Reuben.

Laura had never seen so much food and wanted to sample as many different things as she could manage. She had never experienced barbecued meat before and found she liked the flavor very much. While she was passing a plate of cornbread to Fiona, she noticed Dylan sitting at another table, talking and laughing with some of the other vaqueros from the rancho. When Dylan looked up and saw her, he nodded, but she pretended not to see and continued her conversations with the family. She might have known he would show up where there was free food and a party atmosphere. Although she wanted very much to talk to him, she didn't think this was the time nor the place.

Later in the evening, there were dances with names Laura had never heard of, such as *la jota, el sombrero,* and *fandango.* Fiona explained that the la jota was a courtship dance where the couples hold their arms high and click castanets while they execute lively bouncing steps to guitar music. Laura enjoyed watching the couples as they whirled and stepped to the music, and she marveled at the speed with which they could click the castanets. She also enjoyed watching the el sombrero or Mexican hat dance being performed, though all the stomping and kicking of the dancers' feet left her out of breath just watching.

Slow waltz-like music began to play, and Fiona rose and walked over the where the judge was sitting. Soon, they both moved over to where the dancers were gathering, and a castanet rhythm was beginning. Just then, Dylan appeared at Laura's side and asked if she would grant him a dance.

"Oh, but I can't dance," said Laura. "At least not these kinds of dances."

"You can stomp your feet and clap your hands, can't you?" Dylan held out his hand to her.

"Yes, but—"

"No buts! Come on. It will be fun." He pulled her up from her chair and headed to the dance area.

Reluctantly, Laura watched the other dancers and began to try to imitate their movements to the three-quarter beat of the music and the castanets. It took her a while to master the rhythm of the stomp while putting it together with the hand clapping and all the while turning and whirling around her partner.

Just as she figured she had mastered the dance and was enjoying herself, the music sped up and the dancers moved faster. Then suddenly, the music stopped and all the dancers stood still. Thinking that was a rather abrupt ending to a dance, she was thankful it was over. But just as suddenly, the music began again even faster than before. This routine of stopping, starting, and going faster continued until Laura was sure she could never regain her breath. She nearly collapsed against Dylan when the dance finally ended.

"Now wasn't that fun?" Dylan asked.

"I'll let you know just as soon as I can breathe." Laura doubled over, gasping. "I don't see how Fiona can do that dance so well. Did you see her? She was amazing!"

"From what I understand, Fiona has been dancing the fandango for many years now."

"I guess I never really thought of her being a dancer."

Dylan made no attempt to go back to join the other vaqueros but instead gave the impression he planned to stick around and spend time with Laura. So she decided to take advantage of the situation.

"I'd like to talk to you about something that has come up, but this is not the best time to do that. Could we possibly go riding tomorrow?"

"Sakes alive, look at you! All of a sudden, you're ready to go out riding."

"There's no need to be sarcastic. You know I've been riding quite a bit more. And thanks, by the way, for letting me keep Sophie at Walnut Hill so that I can do more riding."

"So have you learned anything that might be helpful?"

"I've learned some things that bring up more questions than answers, and I don't know how helpful they will be."

"Like what?"

"Let's do this tomorrow. I see the family is getting ready to leave, and I need to go with them."

"You could stay and watch the bullfight with me. I could make sure you get home safely."

"I have absolutely no desire to watch a bullfight with you, or anyone else for that matter. Besides, how would it look if I stayed here with you instead of riding back with the family?"

"It would look like we were keeping company."

"Precisely. And that is why I am going back to Walnut Hill with the family. I have no desire to give the town the impression that you and I are keeping company." Laura turned quickly and went to join Fiona and the children. She had no idea where Ian had gone, but for the moment, she really didn't care.

Chapter 20

THE NEXT DAY, LAURA had Reuben saddle her horse, and she rode out to meet Dylan on the hill overlooking the ocean.

"Where are we going to go?" asked Laura.

"How 'bout we head down to the beach and ride along the edge of the water?"

"That sounds wonderful. I haven't been to the beach yet. I've only admired the ocean from atop this hill."

They found a handy trail that led down the hill and onto the beach. Laura glanced toward the spot where she had seen a couple of men disappear into the hill but could not see anything that looked like a cave or a tunnel entrance. She was about to say something to Dylan when he nudged his horse into a trot toward the water. Laura hurried to catch up with him, though as the water loomed closer, she began to wonder about her eagerness to ride at the water's edge.

"Is this safe?" Laura raised her voice so Dylan could hear over the din of the surf.

Dylan pulled his horse to a stop and waited for Laura to catch up. "For now, we can just walk the horses. They enjoy being in the water, and talking will be much easier."

They walked the horses along in silence for a while, then Laura mentioned seeing two men disappearing into the base of the hillside. "But I didn't see any opening when we rode by there."

"They may have just walked behind some rocks which, from up on the hill, would appear as though they went into the hill."

"Yes, but there are no big rocks in that area."

"Hmm...interesting. Maybe we'll check it out later on the way back. Now what was it you wanted to tell me?"

Laura told him about Ian's strange attitude lately, about his suddenly leaving on a mysterious trip and about what Fiona said about his "little trips." "What do you make of all that?" she asked.

"Not sure about his attitude, but as for his mysterious trips, that sort of fits with some things I've been looking into. Do you know how often he makes these journeys or when he has done so?"

"I only know about the one he just took. He was away a little over a week, though he told Manuel he would be back before Fiona and the girls returned from their trip. However, they returned a few days earlier than expected, so he was not there to welcome them when they arrived."

"And that was just last month?"

"Yes."

Dylan was thoughtful for a few minutes before turning his horse to ride back the way they came, forcing Laura to do the same. Suddenly, he kicked his horse into a lively canter, and Laura had to struggle to keep up with him. When they reached the point where Laura had seen the two men disappear, Dylan turned and rode up the beach to the bottom of the hill. By the time Laura joined him, he had climbed down and was investigating the hillside.

"Actually, there is a narrow entry here that does not necessarily appear to someone riding by. You go on back to Walnut Hill. I'm going to investigate a little further."

"Should I let someone know where you've gone?" Laura looked worried.

"Definitely do not mention this to anyone at Walnut Hill. If you've not heard anything from me within two days, go to the sheriff and tell him where you last saw me."

Reluctantly, Laura mounted her horse and began the climb up the trail toward home. Looking back every so often, she noticed she could not see the opening or Dylan. Just what was he getting into and why did she care?

Back home at Walnut Hill, she asked Reuben to cool Sophie down and unsaddle and feed her. She slowly walked into the house and headed to her room, feeling as though she needed to lie down and consider all the things she was learning. Though Dylan could be quite trying at times, she worried that he was going to be in a heap of trouble. She felt so helpless, and there was no one she could confide her fears to.

As she reached the hallway, she heard voices coming from the parlor. She slowly opened the door and peeked in.

"Hi, Miss Laura. C'mon in." Bridget bubbled. "We're sprucing."

"You're doing what?"

"She means we're sprucing things up a bit," explained Cassie.

Laura walked into the room where Bridget was dusting, Cassie was adding pillows to the stark furniture, and Fiona was bringing some color to the windows with sheers and drapes.

"This is so lovely. You are doing a marvelous job of sprucing."

"I noticed you had added a few touches to this room and thought perhaps we should make this room a bit cozier," Fiona said. "I'm afraid Ian has let everything in this house fall to ruin. Consuela has done a wonderful job of keeping up with things the way they are, but she just doesn't have time for much decorating, I'm afraid."

"Well, I must say she did a fine job of keeping the solarium in good condition. I still can't believe Ian let us use it for the children's classroom."

Fiona turned from adding some books to a small bookcase and said, "I imagine a certain saucy tutor from New England might have had a hand in changing his mind. Good job, Laura."

"I don't know if it was entirely my doing, but I tend to say what I think when it seems appropriate."

"You look worried, dear," said Fiona. "Are you feeling all right?"

"I'm fine. I'm just a little tired from my ride with Dylan today. I think I'll go lie down for a bit."

"Where'd you go?" asked Bridget.

"We took the horses down to the beach and rode along the water's edge."

"How fun. We must all take a day down on the beach as soon as the weather gets just a bit warmer. We'll pack a picnic and make a day of it." Fiona seemed to get excited at the idea.

"Yes, that will be nice," said Laura, wondering whether it would really be nice or if there would be trouble brewing by then. "I'm going up to my room now. I'll see you at supper."

Laura was worried about Dylan. She knew Dylan was capable of taking care of himself and there was nothing to worry about, but for some reason, she couldn't help wondering what was happening. She did not look forward to having to go to the sheriff and telling him that Dylan had disappeared into what appeared to be a tunnel in the side of the hill. That sounded strange even to her.

A couple of days later, as Reuben was returning from work at the rancho, Laura asked him if he had seen Dylan in the last day or so.

"No, Miss Laura, I haven't. I think he's been out on the range with the herd. Is something wrong? Do you need him to help you with something?"

"Nothing's wrong. I just hadn't seen him since we rode down to the beach, and I had a question for him is all."

"You and Dylan rode down to the beach? Do you like him or something?"

"Dylan is a very nice man and has been very helpful teaching me to ride. He thought I might enjoy riding in the surf for a change."

"Uh-huh."

Just as Laura began to think she was going to have to contact the sheriff after all, Dylan came riding in at top speed.

"I was just about to send a search party out for you," Laura said, hoping she sounded more unconcerned than worried.

"I thought you might be thinking along those lines, but I had to attend to a downed cow and couldn't get away." Dylan turned and saw Reuben standing near the stable. "Hey, Reuben, I missed you today at the rancho. How did things go?"

"Okay, I guess. I didn't hear anything about a sick cow though." Reuben frowned.

"I hadn't gotten back to the rancho to let anyone know before you left for the day."

"Oh, okay." Reuben turned and went toward the house, looking back at the two standing there, wondering if something was going on that he didn't know about.

When Reuben was out of earshot, Dylan turned to Laura. "The tunnel I entered goes all the way into the town of Capistrano. There are many tunnels under the town, and it would be impossible to follow them all. But the main one came out behind the old mission."

"What do you suppose those men were doing?"

"I think you saw a couple of treasure hunters I have been hearing about. I'm just sorry I wasn't able to find them anywhere in the tunnel."

"Could they already have left by the time you got there?"

"That's one possibility, but there are entrances to other tunnels where they could have been hiding or that led to some other area."

"So what do you do now?"

"I'm not quite sure."

Chapter 21

LAURA TRIED NOT TO think about treasure hunters and tunnels as she joined Fiona and the girls for a day at the beach. Holding hands with Bridget on one side of her and Cassie on the other, she cautiously stepped into the ocean and let the tide swirl around her feet. Bridget immediately squealed and ran back to join her grandmother on the sand. Cassie and Laura ventured a bit farther until the water reached their calves just below the pantalets of Laura's swimming costume.

"The water is not as warm as I thought it would be," Laura commented. "It is a refreshing contrast to the hot sand though."

"I think it is the best way ever to cool off on a hot day," Cassie said as she sat right down in the water.

Laura ventured a bit farther into the ocean, stopping only when the water had reached her waistline. She turned to watch Bridget and Fiona attempting to build a sandcastle. As she looked beyond them, she thought she caught a glimpse of a man near the tunnel entrance, but the sun was in her eyes and she couldn't be sure.

Just then, Bridget came racing to the water's edge to fill her pail with water and slipped, falling into the ocean. Immediately, Laura raced to be sure she was all right and found her giggling as she made several attempts to pick herself up only to be washed back as the tide receded. With Laura's help, she was able to stand up, and Laura filled her bucket for her so she could return to her castle building.

Once Bridget was safe and Cassie was busily splashing in the water, Laura turned her gaze toward the spot where she thought she had noticed the man, but there was no sign that anyone was there. *I must be seeing things,* Laura thought, and she went to join Fiona and Bridget on the beach.

"You be careful, Cassie," Laura called. "Don't get too far out in the water."

"I'll be very careful, Miss Laura," she said as she ducked her head underwater.

"Yes, I can see that."

"She'll be fine, Laura," Fiona said. "She is used to the water and knows how to swim."

"I always wished I had learned to swim, but truthfully, I'm terrified by the ocean. It seems so big and vast."

"It is always good to have a healthy respect for the ocean, and perhaps you need to learn to swim."

Laura nodded and thought about learning to swim. It probably wasn't as painful as learning to ride a horse. It seemed she had come to this part of the country to teach the children, but instead, she was the one who was doing most of the learning. She was learning to cook, she was learning to ride a horse, she was learning Spanish, so why not learn to swim too?

That afternoon, while Bridget and Cassie were resting from their outing at the beach, Laura decided to sit in the solarium and read. She glanced at the myriad books on the shelves, trying to decide on one to read. She was delighted to find *Little Women* by Louisa May Alcott, *Twice-Told Tales* by Nathaniel Hawthorne, along with several other Hawthorne titles. There was a set of Horatio Alger Jr.'s *Popular Juvenile Books for Boys* and several of the Little Pets series for younger readers like Bridget. However, she could not resist taking down a rather large volume entitled *Stories of the Wild West and Campfire Chats* by Buffalo Bill.

She sat down in a comfortable wicker chaise and began reading. Before long, she had fallen asleep due to her outing in the fresh air and sun. It wasn't until she heard arguing coming from the stairwell that she realized she had been asleep.

At first, she was a bit disoriented and not sure what she was hearing, but soon, it became evident that Reuben and Ian were engaged in another heated argument about something. She rose, put the book back on the shelf where she found it, and left the solarium. As she came through the doorway onto the stair landing, Reuben ran past her and into his room, slamming the door behind him. Laura looked toward the bottom of the stairs to see Ian standing there with an angry and determined look on his face.

"Is something wrong?" asked Laura.

"There is always something wrong when it comes to that boy. It's nothing you need to worry about. I will handle everything in due time." With that, Ian turned and walked out the front door to stand on the veranda and look out over the hillside.

Laura just stood in place for a few moments, then cautiously walked to Reuben's bedroom door and knocked lightly. "May I come in, Reuben?"

"Go away! I don't want to talk to anyone right now."

"Perhaps if you did talk to someone, you might feel better. Can you tell me what happened?"

The door to Reuben's room opened slowly, and Laura went in as Reuben went over and flopped face down on his bed.

"What's going on, Reuben?"

"Oh, he said he's going on another one of his trips and I only asked if I could go along. He acted like I just asked him if I could rob a bank. He's so mean!"

"Well, he probably has business to take care of and you might be in the way."

"To him, I'll always be in the way. I wish my real father had not died so I could go live with him."

"Now, Reuben, is that any way to talk about the man who has been there for you for most of your life?"

Reuben merely grumbled something incoherent into his pillow, and it was apparent he was finished talking. Laura couldn't decide if she should just mind her own business or go see what she could get out of Ian. Taking into consideration his temperament, Laura decided talking to Ian right now was probably inadvisable, so she went downstairs to see if she could help Consuela prepare supper.

During their evening meal, Reuben suddenly blurted, "Father is leaving us again, girls! He has to go on another trip."

Bridget pouted, and Cassie was obviously disappointed by this news but said nothing. Ian hastily explained, "I should only be gone a day or so." As if that would explain everything.

"I still don't understand why I can't go along. I can take a couple of days off from the ranch work. Senor Valencia wouldn't mind."

"The subject is not open to discussion, Reuben. It is not possible for me to take you with me on this journey."

Reuben started to protest again but realized it was useless, so he just put his head down and continued eating his meal. Watching this exchange, Laura couldn't help but wonder what was so special about Ian's trip that he did not want Reuben to ride along with him. Obviously, Ian had secrets of some kind, and if she could figure out what they were, perhaps she could better understand how to handle both Ian and Reuben.

The next morning, following breakfast, Ian threw his saddlebags on his horse and rode off toward the beach. Since Reuben was over at the rancho and the girls were learning to knit with their grandmother, Laura decided to follow Ian. She was determined to find answers to her questions. She swiftly saddled Sophie and rode off in the same direction Ian had gone. She was afraid she had lost him when she noticed him disappearing into the rocks on the beach.

What on earth could he be up to? she wondered. Carefully, she followed him and dismounted as she drew near the opening in the rocks. She tied her horse to one of the nearby rocks and started to enter the tunnel. Suddenly, she was grabbed by her shoulders and pulled back. When she looked up, she found herself staring at Dylan Laughlin.

"Just what in the name of all that is holy did you think you were doing?"

Laura was glad to see Dylan, but she did not appreciate being scolded like some disobedient child. "I was following Ian, and I saw him go into that opening. I just wanted to find out where he was going."

"You have no business following Ian or anyone else for that matter into tunnel openings. You have no idea what could be in there. What would have happened if I hadn't been here?"

"I guess we'll never know now, will we?" Laura did not like to admit that she could have gotten into serious trouble. "So how is it that you just happened to be here to save the damsel in distress?"

"I have been keeping an eye on that opening ever since I discovered that the tunnel leads into town."

Laura looked pensive. "Well, what is Ian doing going in there, I wonder."

"A very good question."

"Do you think he is involved with hunting for treasure?"

"It's beginning to look like it," Dylan said. "Now, I want you to get back on your horse and head home to Walnut Hill. Let me take care of any sleuthing that needs to be done."

As Laura leisurely rode back home, she pondered all that she had seen and heard. Could Ian's trips involve hunting for treasure, and if so, why? He was a successful walnut grower. Why would he need to hunt for treasure? As always, every answer seemed to bring on more questions.

Chapter 22

WITH SUMMER IN FULL swing, the family was busy with picnics at the hot springs or occasionally at the beach. Laura couldn't help thinking about Ian and his trip into the tunnel which Dylan had suggested was being used by treasure hunters. When Ian returned from his trip, he acted as though everything was business as usual, even joining the family on a few of their excursions.

Dylan told Laura he was going into Santa Ana and would probably be gone for several days. She wondered if that meant he was enlisting the aid of law enforcement and whether Ian might be in serious trouble. She couldn't very well talk to Ian about it without revealing her own snooping. She was certain that would not go over well.

One day at the hot springs, Fiona asked Laura, "Is everything all right, dear? You've been looking perplexed for the past few weeks."

"I guess I've had some things on my mind. I didn't realize it was showing on my face."

"You're not ill, are you? Despite your confused look, you appear to be much healthier looking since you came here last August."

"Truly, I also feel much better. I can't believe I have been here nearly a year already. The time seems to have flown by."

"I hope you are not concerned about your position tutoring the children. You've done wonders with all three of them. Especially Reuben. We wouldn't think of your leaving now."

"Perhaps subconsciously, I've been dwelling on what will become of me when the children no longer need me."

"No need for you to worry about that. Your position here is secure for a long as you want it."

"That's very kind of you to say, Fiona. Thank you. I have grown very fond of Reuben and the girls, and I would hate to leave before they have learned all I can teach. I know that at some point they will advance beyond my capabilities."

"Yes, but let's not think about that now." Fiona turned as Ian approached the pool where she and Laura were soaking. "What's wrong, Ian?" she asked.

"I just heard the cannery is closing down."

"Why should that concern you? You don't need a cannery to process your walnuts."

"No, but I had been looking into their processes for crystallization to see if it could be used with walnuts. It would give us another outlet for the nuts we ship."

"Is that where you've been going on your business trips?" Laura dared to ask.

Ian gave her a look that indicated he was not pleased with her question, yet he quickly answered, "Some of them, yes. What is your concern about my business trips?"

"You seem to be gone much more frequently, and the children are curious." Laura could feel the blush creeping up her neck to her face. She only hoped the redness appeared to be from the hot water.

"Are you sure it is just the children who are curious?" Ian stood to leave. "You might do well to concentrate on teaching the children and leave business to me." With that, he stalked off toward the cabins.

Laura looked at Fiona and shrugged as if to say she had no idea what had just happened. Apparently, Fiona chose to overlook Ian's rudeness and said, "I think we've been soaking long enough. Let's round up the children and prepare to head home."

In the ensuing days, news of the closing of the cannery spread throughout the town and was reported in the *Santa Ana Register*. Laura discovered from the article that the cannery had flourished for four or five years but had apparently been beset by problems. The article didn't state exactly what kind of problems, and Laura wondered whether Ian's explanation of working with the fellows who owned the facility had been accurate or just a cover-up.

When Dylan returned from his trip, he seemed preoccupied with his work, and so Laura did not see much of him for a week or so. She asked Reuben if there was something special going on the ranch, but he didn't seem to think so. Laura was curious as to what Dylan had learned about Ian and his mysterious trips but reminded herself of what curiosity did for the cat.

Finally, late one evening after supper, Dylan arrived on the back veranda and asked Laura if she would like to go for a ride down to the beach to watch the moon rise over the water. Even though it seemed like he was asking for a date, Laura agreed because she wanted to hear what he had found out. Besides, the cool air from the ocean would feel so good on a hot evening. Bridget and Cassie were getting ready for bed, Ian was in his study, and Reuben was at his grandmother's playing chess. Laura left a note on the kitchen table and went to fetch her horse, then she and Dylan rode down to the beach.

Once they reached the hard-packed sand near the water's edge, they dismounted and walked the horses. For a few minutes, they walked in silence, and when Laura could stand it no more, she asked, "Did you find out anything about the tunnels or what Ian was doing?"

"Whoa! You like to get right to the point, don't you?"

"I've been going crazy these past few weeks trying to make sense of all that is going on. You are the only one I can talk to about this, and you haven't been around."

"I can see how that might upset you. First of all, I have no idea yet what Ian was doing down in the tunnel, but I definitely intend to find out. I did learn that there are rumors of treasures still hidden in this area, but I'm not sure that is what Ian is searching for."

"What sort of treasure?"

"There have been rumors for years that not all the mission valuables were recovered after they were buried during the Bouchard raid of 1818. Many people believe that some of those things are still buried nearby. There have also been rumors of buried gold at the mission, and so, folks are always searching in the hopes of discovering a treasure trove of riches there."

"But I don't understand what Ian's involvement would be. Surely he doesn't need to discover gold or other treasure."

Dylan was quiet for a few moments, pondering whether he should impart his newly discovered information to Laura. "Can you keep what I'm about to tell you to yourself?"

"Of course. I just want to know what is going on."

"Did you hear recently about the cannery closing?" Laura nodded and Dylan continued. "It seems the two gentlemen who own the cannery have run up against some financial problems. Ian has been trying to work with them to see if there was a way they could work together using their techniques with his walnuts to produce a tasty treat and keep the cannery in business."

"He did mention something like that, but I thought it was just to cover up what he was really doing."

"In addition, the cannery owners heard the tales of buried treasure and have been going into the tunnels underneath the mission in hopes of finding enough to keep them in business."

"Then why on earth was Ian going in there? Does he believe the rumors too?"

"I don't know if he believes the rumors, but I do think he has been trying to help them any way he can, even if that means hunting for buried treasure."

"I'm not altogether convinced Ian would do something like that. Sure, he has been very secretive about his business trips, but searching the tunnels underneath the mission…" Laura shook her head. "I just don't see it."

They had walked far enough along the beach. It was time to turn around and go back the way they had come. As they turned, Laura's horse nudged her from behind, pushing her into Dylan. She looked up, ready to apologize for bumping into him, when he leaned down and gave her a gentle kiss on the lips. Laura knew she should back away, but she lingered just a moment to enjoy the softness of his mouth.

"I...I...I'm sorry," Laura stuttered as she pulled away from him. "The horse pushed me."

"Oh sure. Blame the horse." Dylan's eyes twinkled with mischief. "There is absolutely nothing to apologize for. I thoroughly enjoyed the moment. I've been wanting to do that since the first day we met."

"But I've been so rude to you. How could—"

Dylan fit his mouth over hers and deepened the kiss, holding Laura so that she could not protest, not that she felt compelled to resist at that moment. When they finally stepped apart, Laura hung her head as if ashamed of her behavior. Dylan put his finger under her chin and lifted her face so that she had to look at him. "Don't ever be ashamed of expressing your feelings, especially toward me."

Laura was at a loss for words. She merely mounted her horse and rode back up the beach to the trail that led back to Walnut Hill. Dylan began to follow her but decided it might be better not to push her too far. Despite the breakthroughs she had made during her year in the west, she was still just a shy, retiring young girl who had not yet experienced life fully.

Laura was happy to discover no one was around when she returned to the house. She did not feel up to talking to anyone or having to explain where she had been. She lay awake on her bed for several hours, reliving the scene on the beach. She knew she should not encourage Dylan's advances in any way, but she had to admit she experienced strange feelings that she had never felt before. She had thoroughly enjoyed being held by Dylan, and every time she thought about his tender kiss, she shivered with the pleasure of it.

Chapter 23

THE NEXT MORNING, LAURA dressed and went down to see what was for breakfast. Everyone was at the table eating, but the mood was glum. She couldn't help wondering what issue had subdued everyone this time.

Putting a smile on her face, Laura said, "Good morning, everyone. What's on the agenda today?"

"I have some business to take care of in Santa Ana today," Ian responded distantly.

"We're going over to Grandmother's to learn some more knitting," Bridget said.

"How about you, Reuben? Are you going to the rancho today?" Laura asked as she sat down and reached for a warm tortilla.

"Guess there's not much else for me to do." Reuben put his head down and sulked. Laura imagined he was put out because his father was going off on business again.

"I thought you enjoyed working on the rancho, Reuben. Why the long face?"

"He is upset with me for going to Santa Ana without taking him," Ian explained. "But it is just not something I can do and have him tagging along."

"Why, is it illegal?" Reuben blurted.

"No, it is not illegal, Reuben. But you would not understand what was happening, and I can't be worrying about what you might do when you got bored. I certainly can't have you roaming around the town and getting into heaven knows what…"

"Yeah, yeah, I get it," Reuben said as he rose from his chair and headed out the back door.

"That boy just does not understand that I have serious business to conduct and that I'm not just going for the fun of it."

"Perhaps if you explained the nature of your business, he would lose interest, or perhaps you could take him to town when you are not conducting business," Laura offered.

Ian looked as though he was prepared to reprimand her for her impertinence, but instead, he merely folded his napkin and left the table. Within a few minutes, he bid farewell to everyone and went out to saddle his horse.

After the girls finished breakfast, they headed over to their grandmother's cottage. Laura helped Consuela clear and wash the dishes. She needed to feel as though she was contributing in some way. Maybe she should see if Fiona would teach her to knit, but frankly, she was not sure she could sit still long enough to learn even a basic stitch.

When Laura finished helping Consuela, she decided to go up to the solarium to continue reading the *Stories of the Wild West* that she had begun before. Perhaps that would take her mind off the tension between Reuben and Ian.

As she passed Ian's office, she noticed the door was standing ajar. It was not like Ian to leave his office door open. She imagined he even kept it locked. *He must have been in a big hurry to get to Santa Ana,* Laura thought. As she reached to close the door, something on his desk caught her eye. Looking furtively around to see if anyone was watching, she ventured into the room to have a closer look.

Spread out across Ian's desk was what looked to Laura like a map of some kind. It showed the walnut grove and eucalyptus windbreak, along with the main house and Fiona's cottage. Just beyond the cottage was a plot of land with what appeared to be trees of some sort lined up. In the margin, Ian had noted, "*Oranges—the second gold rush.*"

Laura didn't quite know what to think about her find, but as she contemplated it, some questions began to fall into place. Ian's business trips took on a different meaning, particularly if he was planning to expand to include growing oranges. Laura didn't know if the area was ideal for growing oranges but was certain that Ian had looked into it thoroughly. He was not a man who did anything impetuously.

"I think it is time for some simple explanations," Laura said out loud to herself. She then left the office, carefully closing the door behind her, and continued on up the stairs to read. However, when she reached the solarium, she had lost interest in stories of the wild west and began searching the shelves to see if there were any books on growing oranges.

The only thing she could find was the *Encyclopedia Britannica*, which offered very little information regarding growing oranges, but it did point out that the first orange trees were brought here in the 1700s by the Spanish and planted at the missions. However, in 1870, a woman in San Bernardino was sent two navel orange trees by the Department of Agriculture; and from that, the business of raising oranges created the second "Gold Rush" in California.

Later that evening at supper, the tone was quite subdued until Ian, looking around the table at everyone, said, "I have an announcement to make."

"What is it, Papa? What?" bubbled Bridget.

"What now?" Reuben moaned.

"The reason I went to Santa Ana today was to meet with some bankers to see if I could obtain a loan, which I did."

"Why do you need a loan? Are we broke?" Reuben frowned.

"No, we are not broke," Ian replied with a smile. "In fact, if we were, I would not have been able to get the loan."

"You mean you have to have money in order to borrow money?" Reuben shook his head in disbelief.

"I am going to be planting orange trees out beyond your grandmother's cottage, and I needed some money to get started."

"You're what?" Reuben almost came up out of his chair. "What about the walnut business?"

"We'll still harvest the walnuts and send them to market, but very soon, we will have oranges to ship as well."

Laura listened quietly to the exchange between Ian and Reuben and could hold her tongue no longer. "So this new venture is the reason for so many mysterious business trips?" she asked. Ian nodded and she continued, "Why all the secrecy? Reuben thought…"

"What did Reuben think?" Ian turned to his son.

"I thought you were hooking up with pirates or smugglers or something."

"Oh my!" exclaimed Ian with a hearty laugh. "I didn't want to say anything until I knew for sure I would be able to do this, and there was a lot of planning that had to go into it. Pirates and smugglers—really, Reuben?"

"Well, how was I to know? You kept sneaking off and wouldn't let me come along. What was I supposed to think?"

"I'm sorry I couldn't include you, Reuben. I just wanted everything to be in place before I said anything."

"So you think growing oranges is a good idea, then?" Reuben suddenly seemed very attentive to what his father had to say.

"I was just reading something in the solarium this afternoon that indicated that orange growing was fast becoming the second Gold Rush in California," Laura added.

"Really?" Reuben's excitement was growing. "So what happens now?"

"To begin with, Manuel and I will have to prepare the land, then I will need to purchase the seedlings to be planted—"

"And we'll have our very own oranges!" Reuben interrupted.

"Now slow down. It will take a while before the trees are mature enough to bear fruit. But when they do, yes, we'll have our own oranges."

"Can I help you and Manuel get the land ready and plant the seedlings?" Reuben asked, hoping he wasn't about to be turned down again.

"If you're willing to put in the work, I don't see why you can't help out. After all, this may all be yours someday."

Laura rose from the table. "Well, this has all been quite enlightening, but it is getting time for the girls to clean up and get into bed. Congratulations, sir, on your new venture. I hope it all works out the way you planned."

"Thank you, Miss Palmer. I think the most difficult tasks are behind me now. Perhaps we can plan a little party to celebrate the new venture and to commemorate the anniversary of when you joined us a year ago."

"My, has it been a year already? I'll see what we can put together." She helped the girls clear the dishes and then headed upstairs to put them to bed.

Chapter 24

WITH THE AID OF Consuela, Laura, Bridget, and Cassie put together food and decorations to celebrate the addition of an orange grove to Walnut Hill. There was even a cake to mark Laura's first year as tutor and mentor to the children. A long table was once again set up on the veranda. In addition to the family, Senor Valencia, Dylan, and the judge from the town attended the festivities.

Laura had not seen Dylan since their encounter on the beach. She was not quite sure how to react to his being at the party, but at the same time, she was curious about what kind of progress he had made in his search for treasure hunters. Perhaps she could swallow her humiliation and talk to him later when there were not so many folks around.

Everyone was in such good spirits. Laura was amazed so much emphasis was being put on her one-year anniversary, yet she realized it had been a good year, both for her and the children. As she was about to cut the cake for all to enjoy, Dylan stepped beside her and took the knife away from her.

"You should not have to cut a cake baked in your honor. Let me." Dylan began meticulously slicing the cake and offered the first slice to Laura before handing out plates to everyone else.

"Thank you, Dylan. That is very kind of you."

"Why, Miss Laura, I do believe you are blushing," said Reuben, taking a plate of cake for himself.

"I'm not blushing," stammered Laura. "It's merely very warm today, and my fair skin tends to redden at the slightest provocation."

"And what provoked this particular occasion?" mused Dylan.

Too embarrassed to respond, Laura simply turned and went to join Fiona at a nearby table but not before she shot Dylan a murderous look.

"We have certainly enjoyed your presence here this year. I think you have done wondrous things for the children. I do hope you plan to stay on, at least until the girls have completed their schooling."

"Thank you, Fiona. That is fine praise indeed, though I sometimes doubt if Ian feels I am worthy of it."

"Don't you bother yourself about Ian. He always has his head so far into his work, he really has no idea what goes on right before him."

"I always seem to get on his bad side, especially when I try to defend Reuben."

"I admit he does seem to have on blinders when it comes to that boy, but I believe he thinks if he is hard on the boy, it will better prepare him to go out on his own when the time comes."

Laura doubted his methods were having the desired effect on Reuben but opted not to say so to Fiona.

"Early on," Fiona began, "I confess I had hoped perhaps you and Ian might find a mutual attraction for one another."

"Oh, I don't know…"

"Before you say anything, just let me say that it is plain as day the attraction you have for Dylan Laughlin, and it would appear he feels the same."

Now, Laura was truly embarrassed and had no idea how to respond, so she merely looked down at her empty plate and wondered if she wished hard enough, would she be able to simply sink into the floor and disappear?

"Don't be embarrassed, Laura," Fiona patted her hand. "There is no doubt Dylan Laughlin is an extremely attractive man, and no one faults you for your good taste. In fact, if I were younger…" Fiona let her words trail to nothing when she looked up and said, "Speak of the devil. Here comes Dylan now. I think I'll go see what the children are up to." She rose, gathered both her and Laura's plates, and marched into the house.

"You look like your favorite kitten just died." Dylan sat in the chair just vacated by Fiona. "Did Fiona say something to upset you?"

"On the contrary, she complimented me on the work I've done this past year and hoped I plan to stay on until the girls graduate."

"Well, just let me second that observation."

Again, Laura felt her cheeks getting flushed. She turned a bit to the side, hoping Dylan would not notice. But alas, her hopes were dashed when he said, "You're blushing again, Laura, and don't try to feed me some nonsense about fair skin and the heat."

"I guess I'm just not used to receiving compliments without feeling embarrassed."

"There's nothing to be embarrassed about, and with respect to the other night on the beach—"

"I'd rather we didn't discuss the other night. We should just forget that it happened."

"I'm not sure I can forget it, Laura. It was a very special moment for me, and I was hoping you felt the same."

"Well, I don't," Laura emphasized. "How is your investigation into the treasure hunters coming along?"

"Nice way to change the subject, but it is not going to work until you admit that you enjoyed that kiss every much as I did."

Laura did not want to admit, especially to herself, just how much she had enjoyed the kiss. Still, she wanted to hear more about his search and so decided to bend a bit.

"It was a very nice kiss, but it must never happen again."

"Not sure I can agree to the part about it never happening again. You never know when a soft breeze and pale moonlight might put me in the mood to hold you in my arms and kiss you tenderly."

Laura was glad she was sitting, as she was certain her knees would buckle if she had been standing. She once again tried to steer the conversation in a different direction.

"You still didn't answer my question about your search for the treasure hunters."

"I'm not sure I have an answer that will suit you." Dylan thoughtfully looked off into the distance.

"What do you mean? What about the men in the tunnels?"

"It seems there has been a story going around that a pirate came ashore in the San Juan Point area some time ago and buried between $3 million and $10 million. Nearly everyone in the valley has gone in search of the treasure."

"Has anyone found the treasure?"

"That's the kicker to this whole fiasco. Nothing more than a tarnished silver cross has been located by anyone. There apparently is no treasure, or it was found years before and has disappeared."

"So does this mean you will be leaving the ranchero and returning to Chicago?"

"Would that bother you?" Dylan teased.

"No, I was just wondering. It seems like your time here has been unnecessarily wasted and you would want to get back to your regular life."

"Laura," Dylan placed his hands over hers on the table, "I don't feel my time here has been wasted, and I have no plans to return to cold, windy Chicago. I like it here and have purchased a small plot of land near San Juan-by-the-Sea where I hope to build a homestead."

Laura looked down at her hands beneath Dylan's and said, "Isn't that the area that has been destroyed beyond recognition? Hasn't it been virtually abandoned?"

"Yes, but that's the reason I could buy some land for little or no money. I'm sure the area will boom once again, so my property will only increase in value when that happens."

"You seem like a very shrewd businessman. Will you continue to work as a Pinkerton agent?"

"As a matter of fact, I am retiring from the Pinkerton agency and joining forces with Ian in his new orange grove venture. So you'll be seeing a lot more of me, and I hope to be seeing a lot more of you." Dylan leaned over and kissed her softly again.

Laura could feel the blush coming on yet felt no embarrassment this time. Perhaps things were working out the way they were supposed to. In the end, who could say what the future might bring, but suddenly, she felt very optimistic about whatever was ahead.

Epilogue

A YEAR LATER, THE ORANGE grove was taking shape. Ian had purchased year-old trees to plant that were now only a year or so away from producing fruit. While Ian continued to oversee the walnut grove, Dylan and Reuben tended to the orange trees to ensure the first crop would be bountiful.

Reuben had reached the age where Laura could no longer teach him. Besides, he was getting his education now in growing oranges. Cassie was rapidly advancing beyond Laura's range for teaching. Ian and Fiona had been discussing sending her the following year to a boarding school back east to complete her education. Bridget was still her same eager self and took pleasure in her lessons. Laura wondered how Bridget would feel if Cassie went off to boarding school, but that was something she would deal with when the time came.

Dylan had begun building a small cottage on his property in San Juan-by-the-Sea and would often invite Laura to accompany him to the property, asking her advice about what should be included at various stages. Laura was uncertain why he felt she would know anything about building, but it seemed she almost always had an opinion whatever his question happened to be.

On one particular such visit to the property, Dylan asked her where she would like the sink to be placed in the kitchen. Stunned by his question, she replied, "What difference would it make to me? It's your kitchen. You should arrange it however it suits you."

"I was hoping one day it might be your kitchen, as well," Dylan replied with a smile.

"That's very presumptuous of you, don't you think?"

"Why do you think I have been bringing you along as the building has progressed? I have feelings for you, Laura, and I know you have feelings for me. I trust someday you will perhaps consent to be my wife."

Taken aback by his forthright comments, Laura simply stared at him for a few minutes. When she spoke, her voice was shaky and unsure. "I…I…I simply don't know what to say."

"For now, don't say anything, but I do hope you will think about it. Now, should the sink go under the window or would it be better over there by the stove?"

"Well, if it was up to me, I would put it under the window so you could look out on the backyard where you should plant a nice garden to grow your own vegetables, and maybe plant some flowers too."

"An excellent idea. See, I knew you would know just the right way to do it."

Shortly thereafter, they headed back to Walnut Hill. Conversation was not possible as they rode at a good pace, so nothing more was said about their previous conversation. However, Laura could not help thinking about what Dylan had said. She was not even sure how she felt about it, but she did seem to get a warm feeling when she thought about what life with Dylan would be like. *Am I seriously considering his suggestion?* she wondered.

As they approached the house on the hill, Reuben rode out to meet them. He seemed very excited about something. Laura only hoped he had not had a row with Ian. They had been getting along so well this past year as they worked side by side in both the walnut and orange groves.

"Reuben, what are you going on about?" Laura asked as she tried to make sense of his stammering.

"I just found a small orange on one of the trees. We're going to be rich."

"Slow down there, little buddy. It will take another year or so before we have oranges that can be harvested and sold. Sometimes, it is best to pluck those first small ones and throw them away. That helps the rest of the fruit get started."

Reuben hung his head in disappointment. Dylan gave him a pat on the back and said it was good that he found a small orange. It meant the trees were healthy and had been fertilized properly. It just took some patience to grow oranges.

After the horses had been watered and put away, Dylan and Reuben walked to the orange grove while Laura went to the cottage in search of Fiona. She knew that Cassie and Bridget were helping Consuela make tortillas, and she wanted to ask Fiona for some advice.

Fiona welcomed Laura and put on a pot for tea. She also placed a small plate of cookies on the table. "I want to hear how things are progressing with you and young Dylan. I noticed you rode up together."

"We had just been to his property in San Juan-by-the-Sea."

"Oh?"

"He's been taking me there every so often and keeps asking my advice about things. Today, he wanted me to tell him where the kitchen sink should go. Then, he said the strangest thing."

"Strange how?"

"He said I should have the sink where I wanted it because he wanted to eventually ask me to marry him."

"What did you say, dear?"

"I didn't know what to say. He said I didn't have to say anything but that I should think about it. I didn't know he even wanted to settle down with a family. He always seemed like a wanderer. I was surprised when he bought that property in the first place, let alone that he had thoughts of marriage."

"If you want my advice, and you probably don't, if you let that young man get away and don't marry him, you are not as intelligent as I thought you were."

"But—"

"No buts. He's a good, responsible man with ambition that will take him far in this world."

"That's part of what worries me. What if I say yes and then he decides to take off for parts unknown? Where will I be then?"

"I think it is highly unlikely that Dylan would do that. Do you love him?"

Laura thought for a moment, then said, "Yes, I think I do. I have grown very fond of our time spent together. I just didn't think it meant anything."

"That's where you are wrong. You two were meant to be together, and it's obvious Dylan feels that way too. So if the subject comes up again, promise me you'll say yes."

Laura nodded, but the churning of her stomach made her wonder about rushing into a lifelong commitment with someone like Dylan Laughlin. She wished she could be as sure about Dylan as Fiona was.

"I guess I'll think about it," she told Fiona.

"Just don't think too long. Dylan might not wait forever."

"But what about my duty as a tutor to Cassie and Bridget? I would hate to have to give up teaching them to go off on an adventure that might not work out."

"Who says you have to give up teaching the girls? San Juan-by-the-Sea is only a short horseback ride from Walnut Hill. You could still be here every day for their lessons and ride back home afterward. Besides, Dylan will be spending a lot of time here in the orange grove. Seems like a perfectly reasonable arrangement to me."

"When you put it that way, I guess it could still work out."

"Of course it can, dear. You're not afraid of marriage, are you?"

"Well, maybe just a little. I've just never planned that far ahead to have even thought about it."

"So now you can think about it. I think you will find it is an excellent idea."

Several weeks passed by with no more mention of engagements or weddings or affairs of the heart of any kind. Laura secretly watched Dylan as he and Reuben went about tending to the orange trees. He really seemed to enjoy what he did, and he was excellent at showing Reuben how to prune and fertilize the trees. As time passed, Laura became more aware of her feelings for Dylan and noticed that he tended to share those feelings.

One afternoon, when Dylan had finished his work in the orchard, he came up on the veranda where Laura was trying her hand at learning to knit.

"You look tired, Dylan," Laura remarked.

"It's been a long day, but it's over now and I have a moment to sit and chat. Have you given any thought to our conversation the last time we were at the building site?"

"You mean about where the kitchen sink should go? I still think it should go under the window."

"Not about the sink, silly. I meant about my asking you to marry me."

"Are you asking?"

"Well, I'm not exactly down on one knee, but yes. Will you consider being my wife and living in the home we have built together?"

"We didn't build it together. You built it."

"Why do you think I kept taking you along and asking for your thoughts on various aspects of the process? I wanted it to be something we worked on together."

Laura put down her failed attempt at knitting and leaned forward. "I confess I have had some reservations regarding marriage. I'm still fairly young and don't have much experience of the domestic kind. If you are sure you want to marry me, then my answer is yes."

Dylan let out such a whooping sound that Reuben and the girls came out to see what the ruckus was all about. Dylan grabbed Laura and began dancing her around the veranda with the children joining in.

"What are we celebrating?" Reuben asked.

"We are getting married!" Dylan exclaimed. "Miss Laura and I are getting married."

"When?" asked Bridget. "Does that mean you won't be our teacher anymore, Miss Laura?"

Dylan set Laura on her feet, and she bent down to embrace both Cassie and Bridget. "I will still be your teacher as long as you need me to be."

"Can I be your flower girl at the wedding?" Bridget asked.

"Of course you can, and Cassie, I'd like it very much if you would be my maid of honor."

"Hey, I think we are getting way ahead of ourselves," Dylan interjected. "She only just said yes. There is a lot of planning to do before there can be a wedding. But as long as we're on the subject, Reuben, will you be my best man?"

"Absolutely, whatever you need," chimed in Reuben. "We're here to help you."

Just then, Ian walked onto the veranda and, seeing the gleeful faces of his children, inquired what was going on. The children all began talking at once, but when he finally managed to decipher what they were trying to say, he stood and said, "Miss Laura, it would be my honor if you will permit me to give you away."

With tears in her eyes, Laura sighed, "That would make everything just perfect."

About the Author

AS A CHILD IN rural Ohio, Ruth Flanagan dreamed of becoming a writer. The lack of support from friends and family forced her to pursue other endeavors throughout the years. However, she has written several essays and humor pieces, has published a short story entitled *The Cat's Laugh* in *Cat Fancy* magazine, and has written and edited an online magazine featuring articles about life on the central Oregon coast.

Ruth Flanagan began writing *Secrets of Walnut Hill* when she was living near the San Juan Capistrano area. It has taken nearly fifty years for her to complete it in between being a wife, mother, and administrative assistant. Though she has lived in Ohio, California, and Oregon, Ruth Flanagan currently lives on an island in Puget Sound in Washington where she just retired from eight years of editing a bimonthly magazine for the local senior center.

CPSIA information can be obtained
at www.ICGtesting.com
Printed in the USA
JSHW022027240523
42207JS00001B/84